MITCHELL COLLINS

MICHAEL W. MOUNTAIN

Copyright © 2021 by Michael W. Mountain.

All rights reserved. No part of this publication may be reproduced, distributed, or transmitted in any form or by any means, including photocopying, recording, or other electronic or mechanical methods, without the prior written permission of the author, except in the case of brief quotations embodied in critical reviews and certain other noncommercial uses permitted by copyright law.

Printed in the United States of America.

Library of Congress Control Number: 2021952946

ISBN	Paperback	978-1-68536-226-3
	eBook	978-1-68536-227-0

Westwood Books Publishing LLC
Atlanta Financial Center
3343 Peachtree Rd NE Ste 145-725
Atlanta, GA 30326

www.westwoodbookspublishing.com

DISCLAIMER

This book is a complete work of fiction. Any references to historical events, real people, or real locales are used fictitiously. Other names, characters, places and incidents are products of the author's imagination, and any resemblance to actual events or locales or persons, living or dead, is entirely coincidental.

DEDICATION

I am dedicating this book to my one and only grandchild, William B. Mountain.

CONTENTS

Father Mitch 1
School Days 4
Fitting In 7
Trying Times/Best of Times 11
Eighth Grade At OLPL 16
Eighth Grade 21
The Final Break Up 26
Summertime and the Living Is Unbearable 32
Back Home & Back To OLPL 35
Last Year Of OLPL 41
Graduation & Priesthood 48
Summer with CB 52
Nazareth Hall 58
First Year 63
The Truth 70
Making Amends 79
The Last of Sybil Newman?? 85
Senior Year 89
Almost Out 98
Preparing for Next Step 102
Graduating 105
The Seminary 109
Graduation 113
Graduate School 119
First Assignment 124
Priestly Duties 129
Charitable Works & Ham Dinner 136

Callie Gavrilo 142
Preparations for the Ham Dinner 147
After the Dinner 152
New Life 156
What to do??? 161
Home at Last. 168
On My Own at Last 173
Sybil Newman???. 179
Marriage, Family & Death 183

Epilogue 191

FATHER MITCH

My name is Mitchell Collins or just Mitch and this is my story of being a Catholic priest. I grew up in south Minneapolis and I am currently 69 years old. My life story is probably one of a kind and I'll likely be excommunicated from the Catholic Church for telling you my story.

However, here goes; I was born in 1950 to Bridget and Francis (Frank) Collins. My sister Kathleen or Kit is two years older than me and we have remained very close throughout our lives. Our home was a modest post-war rambler in a blue-collar neighborhood. Most of the men worked and their wives stayed at home with the children. My dad worked for the railroad as a brakeman and worked long odd hours almost every day. As long as I can remember, my family was quite a bit different than other families in the neighborhood. My dad lived in our unfinished basement. When I was about five or six years old, I ventured down the forbidden staircase to my father's living quarters. Much to my surprise, in the unfinished basement was a dresser, a small closet, a single bed, a small refrigerator, a small wooden table and a wooden chair. In the corner of the basement there was a little bathroom with a toilet, sink and shower. There were no curtains on the windows except for one in the bathroom that covered a small basement sized window. It appeared to me that my father lived in poverty when we had all we needed.

As I stated, the basement was the forbidden area of the house. My mother stated in a very vehement way, that under no-circumstance, should my sister or I enter the private domain of the man she called "Satan."

Now, I did see my father from time to time as he entered the backdoor to go down to the forbidden basement. He always stopped and said hello and asked how I was doing. If my mother was not around, I could always respond to him. However, if she were present, I could not even acknowledge him. On the times I could talk to him I enjoyed it very much. He didn't seem like the devil to me and I liked him.

My mother was a religious fanatic, or as I used to call her behind her back, 'a religious nut.' Ever since I could remember, we prayed on our knees with her three times a day, morning, noon and night. We went to confession twice a week, Wednesday nights and Saturday morning. We attended mass twice on Sunday, first at eight o'clock in the morning and later the noon service. When school began my sister and I attended mass every day with our classmates. So, during the school year we attended mass every day and twice on Sunday.

My sister and I were told by our mother, the crazy religious nut, that after grade school we'd both enter a religious order. My sister would enter the convent of the Sisters of Saint Joseph of Carondelet and I would enter Nazareth Hall and after that the St. Paul seminary. My sister was going to be a nun come hell or high water and I would become a priest whether I wanted to or not. Mother said it was God's calling for us.

My sister and I attended grade school at Our Lady of Perpetual Love, or commonly called OLPL, a school that went from first grade through ninth grade. Needless to say, we were overcome with indoctrination of the Catholic faith. When I say indoctrination, what I really mean is brainwashed. We were told what to believe and what not to believe. We never were we able to ask the question, 'why?' If we did ask, 'why,' we were given a slap across our hands with the wooden ruler by the nun.

Living with my mother all those years and going to that school was like existing within a prison. We were not able to form our own opinions or question either our mother or the nuns. My dad was supposed to be the devil or Satan, but it felt like my sister and I were living in hell just upstairs from the devil. When my sister and I were left alone for short periods of time, we talked frequently about what we really wanted to do with our lives. We both agreed we clearly did not want a life of religion shoved down our throat every day. We agreed we'd rebel when the time came to leave our crazy mother.

SCHOOL DAYS

I think I was in about third or fourth grade at OLPL, when I realized that I was beginning to mentally retain things that happened to me. As you grow older, you remember things more vividly than before those ages. That's when it became more and more obvious to me that I was living a different kind of life than other kids. Most, not most, but all of the kids stayed away from me because of my crazy mother. They all had seen her at daily mass. She knelt down and prayed so hard that often times she'd begin to cry. She'd cry so loudly that every head in the church would turn and watch her. It was so embarrassing that I'd lower my head to my chest in hopes that no one would realize that she was my mother. But they all knew. Her performance continued throughout all of my tenure at OLPL.

I was in seventh grade and was walking home alone as usual, when the prettiest girl in my class, Sybil Newman, walked up behind me and tapped me on my shoulder. I turned to see who it was, and I almost wet my pants. I looked her over close up for the first time ever and she was beautiful. She said, "Hi cutie, would you mind if I walked with you?"

I was lost for words. I tried to speak but nothing came out. This was the first time anyone in my class had ever spoken to me. I finally stuttered out the words, "Okay, I… don't… care. Why do… you want to walk with me?"

The nickname that all the kids called her by was just Syb and she replied, "Why do I want to walk with you? Well, it's because you are the mystery boy and you're very cute. You probably don't know this, but all the girls really like you, including me."

"Girls like me. Why? You called me the mystery boy, why is that?"

"All the girls think you're cute and the mystery part is because you don't talk to anyone, not even the boys."

I was still confused. Here was the cutest girl in class, maybe the entire school, wanting to walk with me and I was questioning her motives. I finally said, "I'd like you to walk with me. I think you're pretty cute too. Please don't tell any of the other kids I said that and please if you ever meet my mom don't ever tell her I said that."

Syb smiled at me and said, "I promise I won't tell anyone, particularly your mom. I see her at church often and she is, well, different. I'm not judging her, she's just a bit different."

I laughed out loud and replied, "You think she's a bit different? A bit? She a whole lot different. I call her the crazy religious nut. If you only knew."

Syb smiled at my comments and quietly said, "Let's talk about other things. How do you like OLPL? I think the nuns are too strict. What do you think?"

I replied, "Those old ladies are as crazy as my mother. They call themselves representatives of God here on earth, but they beat us guys with that ruler every time we make a mistake. I don't believe God would beat us like that. You girls have it made; they never hit you."

Syb didn't say anything for quite a while. She finally said, "Well, we have some issues with the priest, Father Boyd. I can't stand that man. He is supposed to be godlike but he's a weirdo. My mom calls him a pervert."

"What do you mean by a weirdo and a pervert?"

"He likes all the girls. Did you ever notice that when we get our report cards, he has all the girls sit on his lap before he hands them the card? My mom and dad have complained to the school principal Sister Anne, but she says he's just being friendly. I hate him."

"You hate a priest? Don't ever say that around my crazy mom."

Syb said, "Do you realize that we live only two doors away? We can walk home together every day. I hope you'd like that; I know I would."

I smiled at her and said, "You bet I'd like that. You are the nicest girl in the class. And you're really cute too." I stopped and thought what I had just said. I quietly said, "I'm so sorry that I said that. It's just that I've never spoken to any girl other than my sister. I'm so sorry."

Syb replied, "Please don't be sorry, that's a compliment and every girl likes compliments. I know you boys don't look into a mirror very often, but you are one handsome boy. As I told you before, all the girls like you and they like you a lot."

I was clearly embarrassed as I said goodbye to Syb. I thought to myself, 'This could be a very good year for me. Walking home every day with Syb would be so much fun. I just needed to keep this a secret from my mom, crazy Bridget.'

FITTING IN

Meeting Syb was the best thing that could have happened to me. She brought out my personality and also help build my confidence. I began to talk to the boys in my class and found that I liked most of them. They encouraged me to try out for the basketball team and they wanted me to play baseball in the spring. I was finally fitting in and having some fun in school.

Syb and I walked home from school every day. When I made the basketball team as a reserve, she waited until my practice was over so she could walk home with me.

I had to be discreet so crazy Bridget wouldn't find out I had a girlfriend. As everyone knows, if you're going to be a priest you must remain celibate. I could never understand why a priest couldn't be married or have a girlfriend, but it was something that the nuns didn't want to talk about. If someone brought it up, they got the ruler across their hands.

Syb was the best and only thing in my life. I couldn't believe she liked me. Sometimes we held hands as we walked and once after it became dark in early fall, she grabbed my hand and pulled me into the alley next to a garage and kissed me on the lips. When that happened, I thought, 'now I knew what heaven was really like.' After that kiss I said to her, "Now I know how it feels to love someone. In my lifetime, the only person I've ever loved is my sister and that is sure different than loving you."

Syb replied, "Mitchell Collins, how can you say that? You must have love for your father and your mother, don't you?"

"Syb, I don't even know my dad at all. I only see him once in a while. And my mother, you know she's crazy, how can I love a crazy person?"

"She's your mother for God's sake, your mother!"

"Syb, she doesn't love me or my sister. Anyone that loves a person does not treat a person as she does. My sister loves me and is so kind to me. And, I love her the same way. You have been the only person besides my sister that I can say I love for real. You are the best thing in my life."

"Mitch, I'm so sorry you feel that way. I really like you, but I'm too young to be in love with you or anyone else, for that matter. Please don't think poorly of me but I don't love you and you shouldn't think you're in love with me. I think we should stay away from one another for a while. I'm sorry but I think I'll just walk home with some of my girlfriends from now on."

Losing Syb was a heartbreak for me. I felt so all alone. My sister Kit tried to console me, but I just couldn't get Syb out of my thoughts. I began to take basketball more seriously, and I thought if I could get really good Syb would want me back again.

I began to make friends with a couple of guys on the team. One kid in particular named John Blevins I really liked. He was funny and always made fun of the nuns behind their backs. I finally had a male friend that I could share some of my problems with. I told him about my crazy mom and he laughingly changed her name to CB, for Crazy Bridget. He was allowed to enter into our house after I lied and told CB that John was going to be a priest. Being a priest was the last thing on John's mind. Actually, a girl named Susie Benton was the first thing and only thing on John's mind, and she was a real looker.

Towards the end of seventh grade Susie Benton was having the very first boy/girl party our class had ever had. It was scheduled for a Friday night and would begin at seven and would end at nine-thirty.

Now, not everyone in our class of thirty-six was invited. Only twenty of the so-called hip-kids were asked to attend and I was not one of them. My buddy John, of course was the first boy invited. John talked to Susie on my behalf and she relented and invited me. I accepted the invitation and knew I had to figure out a way to lie to CB to get out of the house. I knew Syb would be there and she would be paired up with a new kid name Jimmy. I hated that kid and he knew it, but he didn't know why I hated him so.

As I was trying to conjure up a really good lie to get out of the house, my mind turned to God. If I were going to become a priest, I shouldn't hate anyone. So, I asked God to forgive me for hating Jimmy, but I also asked him to give me a way out of the house on the party night. For some reason He didn't answer my request.

I came up with a plan; I told CB that I was going to church to try out to be an altar boy. I explained to her as a seventh grader I would be the next class of altar boys. Her response was, "I'll go with you."

I knew that she would want to come along, so I said, "No way! None of the other boys will have their mothers there and I won't either. Having you there will only embarrass me in front of all the kids and the priest as well."

CB retorted, "If you go, I go!"

I screamed, "You are an overbearing bitch, if you go, I won't!"

CB yelled back, "Bitch! You are an ungrateful fool! Don't you ever use that type of language in my house ever again. You're going to be a priest and priests do not use that type of language, ever! You must become an altar boy and I will go with you."

I had been brow beaten enough by this crazy old lady, so I screamed, "Goodbye Bridget, I'm going without you!" I walked out the door and went to John's house and then on to the party.

John and I got to Susie's party exactly at seven and we were the last party-goers to arrive. We walked down to the finished basement where all the kids were quietly talking. The boys were lined up on one side of the room and the girls were on the other side. The boys were staring at the girls and the girls were staring back at the boys.

I immediately saw Syb and I walked across to where the girls were lined up and said, "Hello Syb, you look really nice tonight."

Right after I made my comment to Syb, someone grabbed me from behind and turned me around and slugged me in the face. I dropped to the ground and a major ruckus began. Jimmy, the new kid, was the jerk that smacked me. My friend John immediately smacked Jimmy back. The rest of the boys jumped on John and the next thing I remembered was Susie's dad kicking everyone out of the house. I was lying on the floor in a pool of blood with Syb holding my hand. Mr. Benton stood over me and said, "Son, I'll need to call your parents and have them come over and pick you up."

I lied, "No, I'll just leave, my folks are not at home."

Mr. Benton replied, "Then I must give you a ride, you are in no shape to walk."

Mr. and Mrs. Benton, Susie, Syb and I got into their car and I instructed the Benton's where I lived. We pulled up in front and the lights were on in the house. The Benton's said, "Good, your folks are home now, let's go and get them."

Our front door swung open and CB ran out screaming, "Where have you been, where have you been? You were not at church, no one was at church. I've been so worried."

Mrs. Benton tried in vain to calm her down and she finally yelled, "He was at our house when he was hit in the face. Susie our daughter, was having a girl/boy party."

CB looked at me and for the first time she realized I was injured. She yelled louder, "A boy/girl party? My son is going to be a priest, he can't go to boy/girl parties. What is wrong with you people, do you not have God in your lives?"

Just as CB was about to scream some more at the Benton's, a figure came out of the shadows and said, "Thanks for bringing our son home. Please excuse my wife, she gets upset very easily. I'm sure the sight of blood on our boy has upset her."

CB just stared at my dad and never uttered another word. Syb hugged me goodbye and whispered in my ear, "I love you too."

TRYING TIMES/BEST OF TIMES

After the Benton's drove away, my dad grabbed a hold of my arm and escorted me into the house. My mother walked ahead of us as my sister looked out the picture window in our living room. Once inside CB was ready to pounce. Her scream was almost out of her mouth when my dad yelled, "Shut the hell up! You'll not treat these kids like this any longer. They want a life, a life that does not include your church every minute of the day. Now, I want you listen to me and listen good; I've stayed away from you and my kids as you requested but that ends tonight. I cannot and I will not allow you to ruin their lives. From now on you kids come and talk to me every day and every night. I want to hear what you're doing and what you want to do. Do you understand that Bridget?"

CB never uttered a word; she just walked into her bedroom and closed the door. I felt a big relief to know I didn't have to explain my presence at a boy/girl party. And, I didn't want to explain Syb and my injured face. I did feel bad for CB. Her world was likely crashing down.

My sister walked to the door to CB's bedroom and quietly knocked. CB said, "Come in."

Kit told me later CB was lying across the bed sobbing. Mom said to her, "God is punishing me for not being able to raise you kids as he wants me to. He's told me you must become a nun and Mitch must become a priest. You are not allowed to do anything else. I'm sorry but that's the word of God."

My dad asked me to come downstairs to his room after I cleaned up. When I got downstairs, he asked me to sit on the bed as he sat in his only chair. He began, "Mitch, I'm sorry I've left you and Kit to try and live with your mother without me. But I did promise your mom I would. Now I've had a change of heart and I want to discuss a few things with you and Kit. Would you please get her to come down here?"

I ran upstairs as Kit was leaving a sobbing CB alone. I said quietly, "Dad wants to talk to us downstairs."

Kit had a confused look on her face and said, "Downstairs? I've never been downstairs. Mother always said I could be attacked by Dad, you know sexually."

"Kit, he's not like that. Come with me and find out for yourself."

When we got downstairs Dad asked us to sit down and after we did, he began his story. "When I met your mom, she was nineteen years old and already had a child out of wedlock. She got pregnant in high school and had the baby her senior year. She never graduated from high school."

I interrupted him, "She had a baby in high school? What happened to the baby?"

Dad replied, "Her folks made her give the baby up for adoption and it's my understanding the couple that adopted the baby were both doctors."

"So, the kid had a pretty good life."

"Yes, I'm sure it did. But please let me finish; I met your mom in a bar called the Cedar Inn in south Minneapolis. She was a cutie and had a great figure. I had heard she was easy, by easy I mean sexually. After having a couple of beers we went back to my apartment and I found out she was indeed easy. But I liked her nevertheless and I continued seeing her off and on. I also knew she was seeing other guys that she'd pick up in the local bars. About six months after our first encounter; your mom told me she was pregnant with my child. That would be you Kit. Now I never questioned how she knew I was the father, but I was willing to accept the responsibility of being a dad. So, we got married by the Justice of the Peace in downtown Minneapolis. I had just bought this house a short time before I found out about you, Kit. So, we moved in and five months later we had a baby. Any questions yet?"

Kit was the first to reply, "You're not sure you're my biological father? Did she have any other guys she tried to pin me on?"

Dad said, "Not that I know of. Keep in mind I had a good paying job at the Soo Line Railroad. Most of the guys that hung out in the seedy bars were unemployed. Also, I had just bought this house. I just assumed you could be mine and I just didn't care, I really liked your mom. I also really loved being your daddy."

"But Dad, I'd like to know for sure. I'm sorry but I don't even know you. Mom always told me to keep away from you. She said you'd try and rape me when I got older."

Dad took a deep breath after Kit's last comment and finally said, "Kit my dear, something like that would have never happened. Please believe me. But let me continue; after Mitch was born, your mom got religion. She went to confession every week and mass every day. She developed a friendship with the parish priest named Father Bernard. He was quite a guy. Big talker and acted very pious. Your mom was infatuated with him and went to confession to him every week and also spilled her guts out about personal things to him. He then encouraged her to come to him for counseling at the rectory. She went every Tuesday and Thursday evenings. She was bound and determined to get God's forgiveness for her past sins. I didn't mind because it gave me time to spend alone with you kids. In those days your mom and I shared a bedroom. But I realized every night she came home from her counseling sessions her hair was disheveled and her dress was wrinkled. So, I did what any good husband would do, I asked her about it. She told me in no uncertain terms that her dear priest was helping her get thorough some of her questions about the Lord. She called it bible study."

Kit asked, "What were her questions? Did you ask her?"

"Kit my lovely young daughter, I didn't need to ask her, I already knew. She was having an affair with the esteemed Father Bernard. After she left for a counseling session one Tuesday night, I had our old neighbor come over and watch you kids. I went to the parish house. There was a light on upstairs, but no other lights were on in the whole house. I knocked quietly on the side door and no one answered. I turned the doorknob and it opened. I crept up the staircase to the room with the light on and peeked inside. There on the bed was the esteemed priest Father Bernard, lying naked on top of your mom grunting and groaning in sexual pleasure. I walked in and yelled, get off my wife you deviate. Your mom had a panic look on her face, but the priest did not. He had the gall to say, 'What is the meaning of this Interruption? We're in a counseling session here. Get out and get out now before I call the police.'"

I sat there in silence, but Kit screamed, "He said get out, they were having a counseling session? He was having sex with our mother; it wasn't a counseling session. What did you do?"

Dad cleared his throat and said, "I grabbed that pervert off the bed and threw him onto the floor. I yelled at your mom to get dressed. I then hit him several times in the face. I know I broke his nose and both his eyes were swollen shut. He was bleeding from cuts over both his eyes. I then stood up and I kicked him in the balls three times. We left him there passed out on the floor and as we walked home your mom kept sobbing that, 'He is a man of God and she was just doing her duty by learning the bible.' I need a beer kids, would you like one?"

Kit said, "Yes, I could use a beer, how about you Father Mitch?"

I said, "Why not? This is more than I ever expected."

Dad continued, "After that I went to the Archdiocese and spoke to a Bishop there. I explained what happened and he replied, 'That's what you say. We were told that you assaulted our priest while he was in a bible study session. Father Bernard has already asked us for a transfer to another parish, just to get away from you. It will take several months for the transfer to take place, so I say to you right now, stay away from Father Bernard. I'm hopeful that Father will not press charges if you leave him alone, but if you don't, Father will go ahead and press charges against you. His good name in the community means so much to him.'"

I smiled after taking several hits off the beer and I confidently spoke up, "And, she wants me to become a priest? She's a sick woman. I hope you plan on staying here with us. It seems we need you more than ever now. I think Kit and I would like to be able to talk to you."

Kit shook her head yes after I made the comment about him staying.

Dad replied, "Yes, I plan on staying. I'll let your mom live here with you two, but she will be kicked out as soon as you two are on your own. I'm sorry I let her go on as long as I did. But I was also working long hours and sleeping most of my time off. I now have more seniority with the railroad, and I can get better paying jobs with less hours. So yeah, I'll be around more."

Kit looked at me and said, "Mitch, we need to be nice to her and treat her well. I'm afraid she is mentally ill, and she might try and kill herself."

I replied, "Naw, she'd never offend God by killing herself. I promise I'll be nice to her but being a priest maybe a long shot for now."

EIGHTH GRADE AT OLPL

The summer was flying by and school would begin in less than a month. I tried to behave when I was around CB, but sometimes it was difficult. I finally was able to see friends and play basketball. I went to confession on Saturday mornings after mass and I only went to mass once on Sunday. It seemed that CB had lightened her views a bit on the religious life. Kit had left for the Visitation Convent in St. Paul to try and become a nun. Our dad told her in no uncertain terms that if she didn't like it, he'd pick her up immediately. It was nice having him back in our lives, but he still was not around very much because of his work schedule.

My life was a different story all together. It was the first time in my life I had friends and we could talk freely about girls, masturbation and all other things sexual. We all had masturbated but before we were afraid to admit it. We all went to confession on Saturday, but none of us ever asked the priest to forgive us about our masturbation. We all figured that God made us this way and therefore masturbation was not a sin. I didn't run that by CB however, I knew if she thought I was masturbating and committing mortal sins, I'd be at confession every day.

I was also back with the love of my life Sybil. We were getting more daring and were fooling around a bit more. She called it petting, I called it feeling her up. One day very close to when school would be starting, Syb ask me if I wanted to go all the way. Now I thought I knew what that meant, but just to make sure I asked her if she meant intercourse. She replied, "Yes, I mean intercourse. I stole some things they call rubbers at the drugstore where I work, and they protect the girl from having a baby. What do you think?"

I asked, "Can I see what you're talking about?"

Syb pulled the rubbers out of her purse and I examined them. They were in a package, but I got the idea of how they were to be used. I quickly said, "I'm in."

Her reply was, "Very funny."

I was a bit confused, but when I finally got it, I said, "I'm in. I'm sorry, I didn't mean that to be funny."

Syb just laughingly said, "I thought it was cute. Tonight, at my house around seven, can you get away?"

"Wild horses couldn't keep me away. Wait a minute, did I say that correctly? Is it wild horses can take me away? Whatever, seven o'clock it is, and your parents better be away too."

"Yeah, my parents will be away, unless you'd like them to see what you're going to do with me."

"No, I wouldn't want your parents to see what you're going to do with me. Remember I'm going to be a priest." With that Syb walked away laughing her cute little butt off.

I told CB that I was going to shoot some hoops down at the park and I'd be home around eight. I laughed to myself after saying shooting some hoops. I was going to be shooting something, but it wasn't hoops. She just nodded and went back to reading her bible.

I was so excited I couldn't stop smiling. I was going to have sex with the girl I loved and no one could stop me. I then thought about Syb's parents, they could stop me. And God, he could clearly stop me. I was over thinking this whole sex thing. I told myself, 'just go for it and worry about God later.'

Ten minutes later I was wrapped up in Syb arms and we were struggling to get each other's clothes off. After reaching her bedroom and then on to her bed, it took all of about two minutes and I was out of breath lying beside Syb. She said in a very quiet tone, "I hope it was fun for you, it wasn't much fun for me. I expected, well, something a bit better than that. I'm not sure I'll be doing that again anytime soon."

I felt so bad. It was so good for me and she hated it. Well hate was a pretty strong word. Maybe dislike is a word I'd like better. I didn't know what to say or do. I slid closer to her and began to kiss her. Syb quietly said, "Mitch, I think it would be best if you went home."

I got up and said, "I'm sorry I didn't please you, but keep in mind it was my first time too. I think if you give me another chance, I can do better."

"Mitch, go home. I'm not in a very good mood right now. I was expecting more than what I got. See you later."

I did see Syb later, much later, well almost four weeks later. She ignored me the rest of the summer. She didn't, however, ignore Jimmy Larson, he was the ass that smacked me in the face at Susie Benton's party. When I saw her walk past my house holding hands with Jimmy, I almost flew out the door to confront them. I stopped at the door when CB said, "I see you're ready to go to confession. I'll be right with you."

Things had gotten better with CB in the last month. She was still the religion freak but not to the level she had been. She was giving me more space after Kit left for the convent. I figured it was because she had reached half of her goal and she had got one of us in some religious order, I would be number two.

I have to admit I liked CB better. She even laughed once in a while and even spoke to my dad when he came upstairs to say hello. We walked over to the church and both went into the same confessional. This was the first time I had ever gone to confession to the old pastor, I had always gone to the assistant pastors, you know the ones that didn't care what you had done. The old guy was hard of hearing and I had heard from the grapevine, that you could hear everything he was saying to the person in the other side of the confessional. And, because he was so hard of hearing, the person confessing had to speak very loudly. If the priest couldn't hear the person in the confessional he'd yell, "I can't hear you, speak louder!"

I knelt down in the confessional and the good priest slid the window open on CB's side of the confessional. She very loudly said the normal 'bless me father for I have sinned, my last confession was yesterday, blab, blab, blab.' However, after her introduction she got right to work. She confessed she was a horrible mother for letting her son get away from wanting to enter the priesthood. She went on and on about me and how bad I was, and she even said my name. She must have been a regular customer of his, for he knew her name and said he'd have a talk with me. She cried and he gave her absolution. I got up before the window to the confessional opened and walked out.

On the way home I quietly said to her, "I heard what you said to the priest. Actually, everyone in the church heard what you said. I also think, one Hail Mary was not enough penance for what you said. If I were you, and I'm not, I'd stop talking to people about what my future is going to be, or not to be. If I ever hear you mention the priesthood ever again to anyone, I will not go to the seminary, I'll run away and get married. I thought you'd finally gotten some sense and then I hear more of that drivel that I told you I didn't want to hear again. This will be the last time I say this, I'll make up my own mind about the priesthood."

I was pissed at CB and Syb. More pissed at Syb because I loved her. How could she just causally walk by my house holding hands with that little mouse Jimmy. I knew that I be fighting him as soon as I got back to school. Some of the kids said he was worried about me. He knew after he sucker punched me at Susie's party, he was lucky I stayed down. He realized I was bigger than he thought, and I clearly am. I had grown over the summer to just about six feet tall and I weighed 150 pounds. I was a pretty big kid for an eighth grader. I was going to kick little Jimmy's ass.

School began September 3rd and we had lots of new kids. Our class size had jumped to over forty kids, all eighth graders. There were some new girls that were very developed and pretty darn cute. There were ten new kids and only two of them were boys. My best buddy John Blevins said, "Isn't it strange that eight of the new kids are girls and all of them are pretty darn good looking? And can you believe the other two are boys and they are both mutts. Could those guys be any uglier?"

I replied, "John, we have twenty-eight girls in our class and only fourteen boys. I like our odds."

John laughed and said, "You do know that we don't have a chance in basketball this year. There are not enough boys."

I just stared at that fool before saying, "Who cares? Just look at the talent on the other side of the ball. Chicks, good looking chicks."

John brought me back to reality, he said, "I know you often times forget this, but you're going to be a priest. Remember, no chicks for you."

That comment brought me back down to earth. Being a priest. Shit, I didn't want to be a priest. I had already committed a mortal sin by having sex out of wedlock. And, I was going to be a priest. I wonder how many guys that enter the priesthood are not virgins. My guess not many. I laughed to myself, I'll be in a class of my own.

EIGHTH GRADE

The first day of school came and went. My sworn enemy Jimmy stayed a long distance away from me, as he should have. He spent most of his time around the girls, particularly Syb. I could tell the girls didn't want him around, but he had no other place to hide. He knew I wouldn't attack him in front of Syb. I'd have to wait until the time was right, but I'd get him.

Syb always nodded hello to me but really nothing more. I looked at her all the time and I lusted over her. When I say I lusted, I really mean I loved her and wanted her back. She was so nice and so pretty. If only we wouldn't have had sex that one time. I'd do anything to take that back. I remember her saying she expected something better than what she got. Damn, I expected something better than what I got too. It was okay, but being so nervous before and after, put a lot of stress on me too.

School wasn't much fun for me. I had expected this to be a great year. I knew that most of the kids would leave OLPL right after eighth grade and go on to the local public high school. I, however, would remain at OLPL for ninth grade and then on to the seminary. Syb told me two years before she couldn't wait to get to the public school. She wanted to meet new kids, both boys and girls. My heart sunk at the thought of her with other guys. It was inevitable I'd lose her. My path in life was celibacy.

One morning on my way to school, Jimmy, my sworn enemy, walked up to me with his hands in the air and said, "Please don't hit me. I'm so sorry I smacked you at Susie's party. I just lost it when you talked to Sybil. I don't want to fight you, but if you want, I'll let you smack me in the face."

Jimmy stood there with his eyes closed and his chin out waiting for the blow. As much as I wanted to deck him I didn't. I just said, "I won't hurt you, but stay away from me. I still don't like you."

Jimmy responded, "Mitch, I do want to be your friend. I'm planning on entering the seminary after ninth grade too, so I'll be with you."

I thought, 'Crap, this idiot will be with me for another three years after we leave OLPL. I guess I'll have to befriend him.'

I got to school that morning after mass and opened my locker. There was a note stuffed in the little vents at the top of the locker. I looked around and didn't see anyone, so I opened the note. It read;

> Hi! You don't know me yet, but I want to get know you.
>
> Please meet me after school near the
> dugout on the baseball field. See Ya

I read that that note over and over again all day long. I didn't recognize the writing but it was some kind of printing. I thought, 'I hope it's one of the new cute girls in the class.'

After school I walked slowly to the dugout and then it dawned on me, 'It's a joke. Those girls are playing a joke on me. I bet if I go to the dugout all the girls will be there laughing their butts off at me. What should I do?'

I walked close to the dugout and saw someone sitting on the bench. I couldn't see their face, but it did look like a female. I walked up and peered inside; there sat Syb. I walked in, sat down and said, "What's all this about Syb?"

She smiled at me and slid close and said, "We have two rubbers left, would you like to use them tonight?"

"I thought you didn't want to see me anymore and it was such a horrible time for you."

"That's why I think we should try again. My folks are bowling tonight and that means we'll have more time to work out some issues. You know we didn't do any foreplay. Women need foreplay."

I sat there wondering what the heck foreplay was or is. So, I did what every red blooded young American boy would do, I asked "What the heck is foreplay?"

Syb grabbed my arm and slid even closer and whispered, "It's where the guy touches the girl all over to get her excited. He's already excited but she's not. It's the guys job to help get her in the mood. Well, what do you say, are you in?" After the 'are you in' comment, she began to laugh hysterically.

It was quite funny, and I laughed too. I replied, "I'm all in. What time should I be there?"

"No later than seven, I won't be able to wait any longer."

I told CB that I was going to the library and I'd be home around eight-thirty. I walked around our block and then straight to Syb's backdoor. She was waiting there with the door open, with all the lights outside and inside off. I quickly enter the dark house and she took my hand and guided me to her bedroom. Once inside her very seductive room the fun began. I won't go into details but believe me when I say I now understand the term foreplay.

After we finished, we laid in each other's arms for a very long time before Syb said, "Now that's what I call making love. How was it for you?"

I sat up and looked her over as she laid naked on the bed very close to me and I replied, "That was the best thing that has ever happened to me. After the first time we did it, I never thought you'd want to try it again. I'm glad we did."

Syb smiled and said, "How about some more foreplay and try it again, we have one more rubber left. And, if you're interested, I can get more of these little things at work. Are you in?"

I laughed and said, "I'm all in. Maybe instead of three you should steal six."

More foreplay than even Syb could stand, She loudly said, "No more, no more!"

I left her house a happy guy but in the back of my mind was an extreme amount of guilt. What I just did was not priestly. How can I become a priest when I love sex and I love Syb? Only time would tell if I could ever be celibate.

It was party time for some of the in-kids at OLPL. Kevin Johnson was having a party and he invited a total of six couples to his house for fun and games. His parents were going on a weekend anniversary getaway and were leaving Kevin and his sister Judy home alone. Judy was in tenth grade and was a loner. He asked her if she would mind if he had a party and he also asked if she would not tell his folks. She agreed and said she would stay in her room.

Unbeknownst to the party goers, Kevin had some contacts that would provide him with some beer and wine. So, when we got there, we were surprised to see the beer sitting in a cooler and the wine on a table. Syb asked me, "Are you going to have some of that stuff?"

I was a bit confused; I didn't know kids our age drank alcohol. But the more I thought about it, I said to myself, 'I didn't think kids my age had sex either.' I replied to Syb, "I guess it wouldn't hurt to try a little bit. What do you think?"

Syb said, "Mitch, my parents would kill me if they found out I was drinking. They wouldn't let me leave the house for a year, if I got caught. I think we should not risk it. I want to keep seeing you and if I got caught, they'd never let me see you again."

That was all it took for me, I said to Kevin and the rest of the party goers, "We're leaving. Sorry, but neither Syb nor I can risk getting caught drinking that crap. Have a great time and good luck."

Syb and I left, and we had some fun without the booze. We stopped at the park and made out for about an hour and then went to Syb's house and watched TV for another hour. I then went home.

The next day Syb called and told me to come over immediately. I did as she requested, and she was all smiles. She and I walked out to their backyard and sat down on some lawn chairs. I asked, "What's going on?"

Syb replied, "Guess what? The cops raided Kevin's house and all the kids are in trouble. All their parents had to come and pick them up and they'll all have to go to Juvenile Court next week with their parents. I heard that Kevin's sister called the cops when she saw the beer and wine. Susie Benton called me this morning and told me what happened. She and John Blevins were late getting to the party and they had just gotten there when the cops came in. She had no idea there was alcohol being served. She tried to explain that to her parents, but they didn't believe her. She's in a peck of trouble. Aren't you happy we left?"

"You'll never know how happy I am. If we had been caught, I would have been locked in my room for a year and only allowed out to go to the bathroom and to church. You are so smart. Thank you, thank you!"

THE FINAL BREAK UP

Things couldn't have been better in my life at this this time. School was going well. I had friends and a girlfriend I loved. CB had relaxed her control of me, and I was seeing my dad. My dad wasn't around very much, and I suspected he had a girlfriend. After working a twelve-hour days, he would come home, shower and leave. If he came home, it was very late at night. He had talked about divorcing CB but said that would break her heart and her spirit. Even though they had no love for one another, the stigma of divorce weighed heavily on each other. Divorce at the time was considered weakness and the inability to work out one's problems. Only about twenty percent of marriages ended in divorce and those that got divorced kept it quiet.

I made the basketball team as a second-string center and was having a ball. John and some of the guys teased me about having a girlfriend and being a priest. They said I'd be the first priest to marry and have kids. I liked that idea and I shared it with Syb. She replied, "I don't think I'd like that one bit. Having my husband devoted to Rome and not to me would not sit well. I'd want my man to be devoted to me and to me only, got it?"

The first day after Christmas break, Syb asked me to walk her home. I told her I couldn't because of basketball practice. She began to cry, so I relented and said okay. As we walked slowly home in the cold and snow, she had said very little until we got to the park. She asked me to clear the snow off the bench so we could sit down. I did as I was told, and we sat down.

Syb again had tears running down her cheeks as she said, "We have to break up and I can never see you again. Something happened to me that changed my life and it has to do with you."

I sat at the edge of the bench and suddenly all the cold air had disappeared, and I was sweating. I asked, "What did I do? Did I say something wrong? Please tell me."

Syb sat up straight with her shoulders back and forcefully said, "I'm trying to tell you, dammit! I was caught trying to steal those damn rubbers. Two night ago, while I was stocking the shelves at the drugstore, I put two packages of them in my jean pockets. Dorothy the pharmacist, caught me. She asked me to follow into her office, which I immediately did. She looked straight at me and said, 'Please take those prophylactic's out of your pockets and place them on my desk.'"

I did as she said and I quietly said, "I suppose you're going to fire me?"

"Dorothy replied, 'No. I do want to ask you some questions. How old are you?'"

I said, "I'm fourteen and will be fifteen in a month."

'Good, that was about the age when I had my illegitimate child. I was fifteen years old and was pregnant. My boyfriend screamed at me it wasn't his kid, I must have screwed someone else. He had used protection. Well, I hadn't screwed anyone else, just him, three times and he wore a condom. A condom and a prophylactic are the same as the slang term that is used for rubbers. Rubbers are not perfect for preventing a pregnancy.'

"I sat there dumbfounded and I finally said, I thought that's why people used them. They're not that safe?"

"Dorothy said, 'Not all the time. With me, one time they didn't work. My folks made me move to California to live with my aunt June. June was the nicest woman I'd ever met, and she helped me through that awful period of my life. When my baby was born, it was a little boy and I immediately gave him up for adoption. I have no idea where he is now, or if he's healthy or happy. I think about him every day and wonder if I did the right thing. I guess I did, because with no husband and no job and being sixteen years old, what kind of life could I have given him? Now I've only told my story to a few young girls like yourself, my hope was to persuade them and you to stop having premarital sex.'"

"I gulped and began to cry, I said, I'm so sorry for what you went through and I don't want to go through that myself. I'm sorry for stealing, but more important than that, I'm sorry for having sex at my young age. I knew it was wrong, but I love him so much."

"Dorothy quietly spoke, 'Sybil, if he truly loves you, he'll wait until you get married to make love with you. Did you notice I said make love, not sex, there's a big difference?'"

"After Dorothy stood up, so did I, I walked to her and embraced her. We held each other tightly in our arms. We both cried for a very long time as we held on to one another. When we were through, I told her I wouldn't make the same mistake again."

"So, this all comes down to you. We will not have sex ever again. If we were to have sex again, we'll be married. The likelihood of that happening is very remote and you know it, since you'll be a priest. This means that you and I are no longer a couple. I want to remain your friend but not as a girlfriend. This will be very hard on me but it's for the best."

After Syb's last comments she got up and walked away and out of my life.

How about that story old Dorothy told Syb? Well, not a story, but what a truthful, gut wrenching tale. That poor little boy. I hope and pray he's happy. I wonder if my story would have been better if CB would have had me adopted out. Maybe a couple would have loved me and wanted the best for me. I'll never know.

It was hard not communicating with Syb. She said she wanted to be my friend, but it appeared to me that wasn't in the cards. She never spoke one word to me after that. To my surprise my best friend John Blevins and Syb were boyfriend and girlfriend. They went to the parties together and talked to each other all the time, like Syb and I used to do. It broke my heart, but there was nothing for me to do but take it. John and I never talked after that. He ignored me as did most of the other kids. The only one that still wanted to be my friend was Jimmy and as I said before, I couldn't stand that little drip.

School was going to be let out on June 1st and everyone except me had a summer job. I was going to the seminary for the summer to learn how to be a priest. My companion would be none other than Jimmy.

Two days after school let out for the summer and just before I left for my summer indoctrination, my father Francis Collins died of a massive heart attack. It was a big surprise for me, and I cried my eyes out. Even though I didn't really know the man, I did love him in some kind of strange way. After I got to know him, I could tell he was a good man. Had he not been strapped to CB; he would likely have had a good life. My sister Kit came home for the funeral wearing her rookie habit. It would be a long while before she took her final vows, but she still wore the uniform.

Kit, CB and I all sat together at OLPL where the funeral was held. There were lots of people there and I knew none of them. Most were guys from work and from the bar he hung out at. However, there was one lovely lady that sat just behind us. I wondered if that was Dad's girlfriend.

After going to the cemetery and putting Dad in the ground, we all went back to our house for refreshment and to talk about how wonderful my dad was. The lady that sat behind us came up to me and said, "I'm so sorry for your loss. Your dad was a wonderful man and I loved him so."

She then embraced me in a long hug, and said, "You know, you look so much like him."

After the embrace I looked at her and she had tears running down her face. I said, "You were his girlfriend, weren't you? I'm Mitch, and believe me when I say this, you were so good for him. He didn't get any love from my mother."

"My name is Judy Schubert and yes, I was Frank's girlfriend. We were together for over ten years. When your mother went off the deep end, we found each other. I was in a horrible marriage and my husband beat me severely at the ballpark one afternoon. Frank came over and beat the crap out of him. The police came and took my husband away. He's in prison now and is doing a thirty-year sentence for manslaughter. After that Frank and I got together. Please don't think poorly of me. We were just two lonely people that found comfort in one another."

I smiled and said, "Come with me, I want you to meet my sister Kit." We walked to where Kit was standing, and I introduced Judy.

Kit walked right into Judy's arms and they embraced. Kit said, "Dad told me about you before I left for the convent. You were the love of his life. Thanks for being so good to him, it means a lot that you came here today."

Judy tearfully said, "I know I'm not welcome here, and I don't blame your mom for that. Just remember I loved your dad with all my heart." Judy turned and walked away.

As soon as she was out the door CB walked over to Kit and I and said, "That whore, she has lots of guts coming here. I should have kicked her out, that slut."

Kit quietly said, "I liked her. And so did Dad. I'll pray that she finds someone else that makes her happy."

I replied, "Yeah, I liked her too, she's nice and no slut, that's for sure. Mom, you had your chance to love Dad, but you went after the priest instead. I guess that makes you a slut and maybe a whore. Did the good father pay you for the sex you gave him?"

CB was almost hysterical, she stuttered, "Who... told... you... that? You think I... the priest? I bet Frank told you that. Well, I was only doing what God asked me to do, go to bible study. You can call me a slut or a whore, but I know the truth, that priest was just conducting a bible study class."

I smiled and curtly responded, "Well, thank God for that! Now I know I'll never be lonesome in the priesthood. I'll always be able to find comfort in a woman's arms. So much for celibacy. I guess Rome hasn't gotten news of that yet. I'll tell all the priests at the seminary it's okay for all of them to screw. And Kit, I assume it will be okay for you to have a man occasionally in your life. Boy, things are looking up."

CB turned and walked away as Kit and I laughed hysterically. Suddenly she stopped and turned, she said, "You know nothing of what happened in the rectory that night. All I can say is, don't believe everything that father of yours told you. He was the loser, not me. That's all I have to say on the subject. Now you can go back to laughing at me."

SUMMERTIME AND THE LIVING IS UNBEARABLE

I didn't know how CB could live without my dad's income, so I asked her. She smiled and said, "I get his pension and Social Security for you. The house is paid for, so we have no worries."

I sarcastically said, "And he was so mean to you. He left you his house and his pension. Yeah, he was quite a jerk. I hope you enjoy the fruits of his labor, since you never did a thing in your life to make a red cent."

CB screamed back at me, "I stayed at home and raised you kids, that's what I did to earn his house and pension. Someday you'll realize that he was not the saint or the man you think he was."

"I wish you would have had a job and left Kit and I alone." I then walked away.

A few days after we buried Dad, Jimmy's dad drove us to Nazareth Hall in Saint Paul. Nazareth Hall was the high school preparatory seminary that stood on the banks of Lake Johanna. It is where I go after OLPL to get my high school education. It would also be where I'd get my first two years of philosophy. I'd need four years in total of philosophy education and the other two would be at the Saint Paul Seminary.

Summer at Nazareth Hall at first was dull and not very exciting. The priests and nuns were nice and instructed us on prayer, study habits and more prayer. I did like the camaraderie of the other kids. Some other of the potential priests had been at the Hall for all four years of high school and would move on to attend the St. Paul Seminary the next year. They would attend The College of St. Thomas, where they would take the final two years of their philosophical education and also complete their undergraduate degree.

We studied the Catholic bible, which I had never done before and the history of the Catholic Church. I read in amazement that the Catholic Church claims that its bishops were ordained in an unbroken line of succession to the original Twelve Apostles.

We also worked in the Hall as clean up boys. We were assigned jobs and we were expected to complete them on time and the job was to be done in good order. I was assigned to the kitchen and found it to be relaxing and I enjoyed the solitude of the job. I washed dishes and cleaned. It took my mind off Syb, for at least for a short while. My thoughts always came back to my major concern, 'did I really want to be a priest?' I guessed none of these seminarians or potential seminarians, ever had a girlfriend or boyfriend or ever had sex. Now, I knew they all had masturbated, and they were continuing to do so in the dorm's bathrooms. All you had to do at night was find an empty bed and quietly go and listen at the door to the bathroom.

I did mention seminarians and their boyfriends. I wasn't sure, but I assumed some of the boys were homosexual, a term I looked up in the dictionary. It read, 'Characterized by sexual desire for those of the same sex or oneself.' I didn't quite understand it, but I accepted it. Most of the kids that I thought could be homosexuals were pretty nice kids. I figured that the seminary was a great place for kids like that. In my school, boys that were different, were picked on continuously by the more outgoing athletic boys and sometimes the girls. I hated that stuff, but I was always afraid to do anything about it. I feared that they would disassociate themselves with me because I defended the weaker kids, something I didn't want. You see, I was such of an outsider myself, I didn't need any more pressure on me socially. In retrospect, now that I was studying to be a priest, I realized I was wrong. I should have befriended them and supported them. I made up my mind that when I returned to OLPL I would change my ways.

After a couple of weeks at the Hall, I began to enjoy it. The work wasn't hard, and it became kind of fun with all of us potential seminarians teasing each other constantly. Jimmy and I started to become good friends. I had judged him incorrectly as I did lots of people in my life. I realized that everyone is different, and everyone deep down has a good soul. Jimmy and I roomed together, and we talked about everything, including Sybil. He asked me point blank one evening if we had sex. I just stared at him before saying, "Jimmy, if I had sex or if I didn't sex with Syb, I wouldn't tell you or anyone. It would be a private issue. Now, with that being said, did you have sex with Syb?"

Jimmy smiled and said, "Yeah I did. She was a bit scared at first but on the second time she wasn't. She really liked it and I have to say it was pretty darn good. That was the reason I hit you at the party. I didn't want you or anyone else to have the enjoyment I had with her. You see Mitch, I fell in love with her. Now I don't know if it was love or lust, but I sure had something for her. After I hit you, she would even talk to me, let alone have sex with me again."

I was in shock and I had to dig deeper. I asked, "What kind of protection did you use? You did use protection, didn't you?"

"Oh yeah, we used protection alright. Syb got some skins from the drugstore. I think she stole them. I had never heard the term 'skins' before but that's what she called them."

I questioned him again, "Where did you go to have this sexual encounter?"

He answered quickly, "At her house, in her bedroom. Her folks were out, I think they bowled in some kind of league. We were all alone and took our time. I'll never forget it. She has such a beautiful body."

That conversation was a heart breaker for me. Well, it was another heart breaker in the story of my love for the fair Syb. Now, I realized I wasn't the first or the last to have sex with Syb. She was likely having sex with my ex-best friend John Blevins. The conversation with Jimmy put me down in the dumps for the rest of the summer. I heard in movies and on the radio, that your first love was the hardest to get over. For me it was my first and last love altogether. I was going to be a priest and as we say in the seminary, 'no sex for you!'

BACK HOME & BACK TO OLPL

I left Nazareth Hall on August 28th and headed for my dreaded home. Jimmy's dad dropped me off in front of my house and I grabbed my duffel bag from the trunk and walked towards the house. The door flew open and my sister Kit ran out to greet me. She looked very different than the last time I saw her at my dad's funeral. She was wearing jeans and a tee shirt, not the nun's custom. She jumped into my arms and cried. I held her close and said, "Kit, what's wrong?"

Kit pulled away a bit and smiled while tears rolled down her cheeks, she said, "I did it! I did it! I'm out of that damn convent. Oops, did I just swear? I'm so sorry Father Mitch. Mitch, I quit and I'm so happy. I hated it, I hated it."

I replied, "Thank the good Lord, I knew you were not cut out to be a nun. How did CB take the news?"

"I got home two days ago, and she hasn't left her bedroom since that night. She's not dead yet, I check on her every few hours. She just lays on that bed and cries."

I laughed and said, "We better bring her some food and water. Maybe if we're lucky she might stay in that room forever. What do you think?"

Kit smiled before saying, "We could never get that lucky. I'm going to finish high school at Roosevelt this year and then on to college at St. Catherine's. I went over to Roosevelt yesterday and got signed up. At St. Cate's I'm going to study nursing or teaching. I just hope CB will let me live here with you. I need to have you back in my life and I want you to introduce me to some cute guys. I missed male companionship so much."

"I feel your pain sister. I missed female companionship so much I was going out of my mind. I have no idea if I have what it takes to be a priest. I'm not sure celibacy is in my blood. I kind of like a woman's touch."

Kit said, "I understand. Give it a year or two before you decide though. Now how about Syb? Is she still your main squeeze?"

"Sad to say no! She dumped me for John Blevins. I also found out she was seeing a few others too. Kit, I loved her so. I've been beside myself since it happened."

"I've heard love is tough. But, with that being said, I want someone to love and to love me back. I want to try sex and I want a real boyfriend, but not necessarily in that order."

I laughed out loud before saying, "You little slut. I'm going to tell CB what your plans are."

"Don't you dare. I want to live here at least to finish high school. After you go away, I'll have one year alone with CB. Please pray for me. I hope she's doesn't kick me out, I need a place to live at least through high school. Will you talk to CB and get her to let me stay?"

"You know I will. Maybe you can stay downstairs in Dad's apartment, I understand it's very cozy."

"You jerk."

I replied, "Kit, it's so nice that you're home. I've finally got someone around here to talk to. I will convince CB to let you stay. If she won't, I'll tell her I won't become a priest. That will swing her around. Let's make her a sandwich and get her some milk."

We knocked on CB's door and we heard a quiet, "You can come in Kit."

I replied, "How about me, old lady?"

Mom sprung out of her bed and ran and opened the door. She ignored Kit and jumped into my arms. She cried and cried. I finally said, "Mom, it's okay, I'm home for the school year."

CB yelled, "She quit the convent, can you believe that Mitch? She upped and quit. Why would she do that Mitch? God wants her to become a nun."

I tried to calm her down, but she just wouldn't listen to my calm voice, so I did what every red-blooded American kid would do, I screamed, "Shut up with that phony crying and carrying on! You are so out of line here. Kit doesn't want to be a nun. Can't you get that through your thick skull. She wants a home life with a man, not a life of solitude. A life with a husband and children, what in the hell is wrong with that. You should be proud of her at least giving it a try for your sake."

CB tearfully said, "But God told me she should become a nun. It's his will and his will should be done."

Kit finally stepped in and quietly said, "Mom, I was not cut out to be a nun. You see, I have the same wants and desires you had as a young woman, I like men and I want one in my life. That's what you wanted and that's what you did. You had sex early in life and often. I might also add without being married. So, don't judge me poorly, just judge yourself, I'm a product of you."

I backed Kit up with, "Yeah Bridget, you were quite the whore hound yourself. Remember Dad told us all about you and your desires. I will say one other thing on this topic, maybe, just maybe, God really wants you to become a nun. Go to a priest, a good priest that doesn't want your body and confess to him that God wants you to be a nun. The Church will make sure your wishes and your dreams will come true. Now you ask, How do I know all of that crap? It's because I'm going to be a priest."

CB eyes lit up, she said, "Really, you think they'd take me?"

I said, "Yes, of course they would. Just don't tell them about the illegitimate child you had and how you gave it up for adoption. Also, don't tell them you really don't know who Kit's father is. Also, don't tell them about the priest you had sex with. I guess if you don't tell them about your past, they'd have to take you."

CB turned and laid across her bed and said, "Please get out of my room, I want to be alone. You two don't know one thing about my life."

I laughed and replied, "Isn't it strange you want to be in bed alone? In the past you always wanted a man with you."

Kit said, "Mitch, that was uncalled for. Let's leave Mom alone."

We walked out of the bedroom and I had a smile on my face, for it was the first time I had gotten that off my chest. I knew I'd regret it later but for now it felt good.

School began on September 3rd and the class size had shrunk to twenty-two. There were nine boys and thirteen girls. Out teacher was Sister Felicia. She was a rather large woman, around fifty years old and always wore a friendly smile on her face. I figured the school had a friendly teacher for the ninth graders so they could at least have one fond memory of good old OLPL.

Sister was as nice as her smile. She worked hard with the slower kids and gave the more advanced kids a harder curriculum. She was fair with everyone and had no favorites. All the other nuns gave special treatment to the students that were the brightest or that were going into a religious order after ninth grade, but not Sister Felicia.

I went to see Sister after school one day in early October to ask her some questions I had about the Catholic faith. I sat at a front row desk and began my rehearsed questions, "Sister, why is it that students cannot ask questions about the church's doctrine? It seems every time I ask a question contrary to the church's beliefs, I get shouted down and I am told not to question the Catholic church's teachings."

Sister listened quietly to my question and said, "Mitchell my dear, you have been talking to the wrong people. I question the church's teachings all the time. There are things that I just don't believe in, but I do believe in Jesus Christ and his teaching. I know that everything the Vatican says, are sometimes hard to believe and I refuse to believe in all of it. I now keep my thoughts and my questions to myself most of the time, but God knows I question lots of the teachings."

My reply startled her when I said, "I'm considering not going to the seminary next year. I don't think I'm cut out for the priesthood. Also, I like girls. I like girls very much and I've had intercourse. What do you think of me now?"

Sister smiled and said, "I like you more now than before. You are human. Man was made to reproduce, it's in your genes. And women were made to want to bear those children. Its Gods wish. Mitchell, it doesn't surprise me you've had sex before. You are a handsome, intelligent young man and I'm sure there are many girls interested in you. But the priesthood is only something you can decide on. Take your time about the decision you will make, for it will change your life in so many ways. And as far as having sex before you make a life changing decision, it's a good thing in my mind. At least you know what it's all about."

I looked at this wonderful woman and said, "You are the first person that has ever given me a straight answer and helpful advice. Thank you so much, you have lifted a large burden off of me. I'm not going to make any decisions until the end of this school year."

Her reply was, "Mitchell, when I was young, I was a very large, homely girl that grew up on a farm. We had a one room schoolhouse that I attended for eight grades, before transferring to a small high school. My high school graduating class had a total of sixteen kids. I never had a date in my life, and I didn't want a date. I didn't really like the boys and it wasn't because I liked girls better. I was just non-committal to either sex. The only way for me to go to college was the convent. So, I joined when I graduated from high school. It was a means to an end for me. I got fed, and as you can see, I like to eat. But it was a way to get my education and become a teacher. I love what I do and having kids like you come to me and express themselves to me, is the best part of being a nun and a teacher."

I said, "I know why you teach ninth grade here. It's because the first eight years here are pure torture and you make the last year something to remember."

"I know that they want me for ninth grade too. They think I can relate to the older kids better than most. But I feel that I can relate to all kids if a teacher just gives them a chance to express their feelings."

"Thanks Sister, for your help, you never know how much I appreciate this talk."

"Mitchell, you'll never know how much I appreciate this talk. Good luck in making your decision and please let me know when you do."

"You'll be the first person I tell." I got up and left Sister sitting at her desk with a smile on my face. It was the best I've felt in years."

LAST YEAR OF OLPL

I was walking home from school late one afternoon after basketball practice, when a car drove slowly by and kid inside yelled, "Look it's the wannabe queer priest from OLPL." The kid driving then stuck out his middle in the air at me and yelled, "Asshole!"

As the car rolled by, I saw who was driving, it was none other than my former best friend John Blevins. Sitting beside him in the front seat was my lost love Sybil. In the back seat was a boy and a girl I didn't know. I watched the car stop two blocks away in front of Syb's house, and she jumped out and ran into her house. I wondered if she was laughing along with John as he called me the wannabe queer priest. I thought the slang term of queer meant homosexual. She of all people should know I'm not a queer or a homosexual.

I continued to walk down the street and was in front of Syb's house when she walked out. She said, "Can I talk to you?"

I replied, "Why on earth would you want to talk to a wannabe queer priest? But yeah, you can talk to me."

Syb walked closer and I could tell she had filled out a bit in such a good way. And believe it or not, she was more beautiful than ever before. She looked me over and said, "You are more handsome now than ever before and you were always so good looking. And, you've even gotten taller. I miss you so."

I said, "Thanks for the compliment, you look pretty cute yourself. What's up?"

Syb replied, "Thanks, but I'm probably the last person you want to talk to. I'm so sorry if you feel like that."

"Not at all. It's nice to see you, it's been a long time. I see you're dating little Johnny Blevins; you can do so much better."

"I'm dumping him and I'm dumping him on the phone tonight. I can't believe he yelled that crap at you. I can't stand him anymore. He's such a jerk. He is not popular at school and one of the juniors beat the crap out of him a couple of weeks ago. He called the kid's girlfriend a 'mutt.'"

I had to laugh at that story, I said, "A mutt? You're right he's a jerk."

Syb laughed in return before saying, "Would you, or could you, will you, go for a walk with me tonight? I want to tell you some things and apologize to you."

I said, "Yeah, I'd like that too. I do have a question to ask you too. How about seven, I'll knock on your door."

The colder weather was settling in and I didn't think the walk with Syb would last very long. I knocked at her door and she had her coat on and was ready to go. I looked directly into her eyes and saw what I thought was the most beautiful woman God ever put on this earth. She asked, "What's wrong, do I have something on my face?"

I said, "No, I was actually looking at your eyes, they are so striking. Okay, what is it that you want to talk about?"

"First off, I'm so sorry the way I broke up with you. I know you were hurt, but so was I. I also know that me going out with who you referred to as little Johnny, was the wrong thing to do. But I want to assure you that we did nothing like you, and I did. I kissed him a few times, but I never made out with him. Please believe me."

"Well, I do have a question of you and if you don't want to answer the question I'll understand. Did you and Jimmy Larson ever have sex?"

"Jimmy Larson? Little Jimmy? Are you crazy? Did he say we had sex? There is no way on God's green earth that I would ever have sex with little Jimmy Larson. You are the only person that I had sex with, you and you only. And going forward, unless I'm married to that person, I'll not have sex with them. But I need to know why you asked me that question."

"I don't know if you know this, but I spent the summer at Nazareth Hall as the precursor to entering the Hall full time next year. Jimmy also spent the summer there. One night he explained to me that he had sex with you. The reason I'm asking you this, is his story made sense. He said you stole some skins from the drugstore and had sex at your house while your folks were bowling in their league."

Syb had a very confused look on her face as she said, "Skins, what the hell are skins?"

"That's what I thought! I asked him about the term 'skins,' and he said that's a term for rubbers. I never, ever, heard you use that term, but he said that's the term you used. He said the sex was great and you really liked it. My world came crashing down after that."

Syb said, "I know exactly where all that crap came from. Susie and I had a long talk after we broke up about sex. She asked me point blank if I ever had sex with you. She surprised me and I told her we had. She asked where, when and how. She must have told that little shit Jimmy about it and he put it in a story about himself. I had a big argument with Susie, and I haven't talked to her in months. Wow, she sure got even with me. Mitch, you must believe me."

"I do, I do. Let's sit down at the park and talk some more. It's so nice seeing you again."

"It's so nice seeing you too. I really missed you. Mitch, if you ever drop out of the priesthood and if I'm still single, could we try and have a love affair again?"

I laughed and said, "I was going to ask you the same thing. Yes, yes, and yes."

We sat and talked in the cold for over two hours. It was the best of times for me. And finding out the Jimmy didn't score was the best thing I could have heard. Now I knew I was going to beat the crap out of him. Syb and I kissed goodbye and that kiss lasted for a very long time. I was sure it was the last time that would ever happen again.

School was wonderful at OLPL this year. Sister Felicia was the best. I had many talks with her in private and I also had some confrontations with her in the classroom. She always kept a cool demeanor and it seemed she was always happy to have someone challenge her. For the first time as a Catholic, I was able to ask questions and not get hit by that awful ruler.

I continued to play basketball, but we were so bad it wasn't much fun. There was a little girl named Leanna Johnson that came to every game and she smiled and cheered every time I made a shot. That was the only time at a game she would show any emotion. She was the clearly the prettiest girl in the class and was new this year. She lived close by and I saw her almost every day walking home alone. She didn't know any of the kids in school very well, being new and all, so I decided to get to know her. I ran ahead to catch her and lightly tapped her on her shoulder. Before she turned around to see who was doing the tapping she quietly said, "I hope it's you Mitchell Collins."

I said, "Yeah, it's me Mitch. How'd you know it might be me? Can I walk with you?"

She turned and a big smile appeared across her face, she said, "You finally got the nerve to say hello and talk to me. Boy, are you slow? I've been trying to get your attention since school began."

I smiled a bit shyly and said, "I'm not the most aggressive guy in the school, but I'm not the slowest either. It's nice to formally meet you Leanna."

Leanna replied, "Formally? Wow, you are smooth, formally? I'm just teasing, you look like a little boy when you get flustered. Come on, smile, it's called teasing."

I did have a very large grin on my face, she was so cute and very funny. After getting over my shyness I finally said, "You like to tease. I came from a family that doesn't tease much and we didn't know how to have fun."

"Well that's part of the fun having a boyfriend, we can tease each other without having either one getting mad. I can see by the look on your face you were confused when I said boyfriend. Well Mitchell Collins, I'm determined to have you as my boyfriend."

I laughed and I thought to myself, 'I like her.' But I immediately thought of the seminary and the priesthood. I said to myself, 'What the hell, that's a long way off.' I finally responded, "Boyfriend? You are one aggressive lady. So, you want a boyfriend and I'm supposedly him. If you don't mind, I'd like to get to know you better before we have the status of boyfriend and girlfriend."

Leanna laughed and laughed. She bent over and dropped slowly to her knees she was laughing so hard. She looked up at me with tears in her eyes and said, "I was only kidding you. Boy are you slow. Please don't be offended, I like you, but I was only teasing you about the boyfriend crap. The last thing I want is another boyfriend. I would like to get to know you better. I've heard all about you from the other girls. You are the dreamboat of all the girls. Now don't be mad at me."

I could not figure this girl out. My guess was she was just pimping me. I wanted to run away and hide and that's what I began to do. I walked past her and sprinted home. I didn't hear a word from her as I passed by her. When I got home, I went directly to my room. Kit asked me if everything was okay, but I never answered her. I realized I was embarrassed by what Leanna said to me. As I laid on my bed looking at the ceiling, I heard a soft knock on my bedroom door. A voice said, "Mitch, it's me Leanna. Can I come in? Your sister let me in to see you."

I opened the door and Leanna slid in. She set her books down on the bed and stood on her tiptoes and kissed me on the lips. It was one of the best kisses I've ever had. When the kiss was completed, she said, "I'm so sorry I teased you. I Promise I won't tease you this much again. I've been waiting from the first day of school to meet you and when I finally do meet you, I screwed it up."

I said, "Let's get out of here and walk to the park. I really don't want my crazy mother to ask about you."

Leanna quickly said, "Let's go to my house, no one's home. I'll cook us dinner."

We began to walk out, and I stopped and introduced Kit to Leanne. Kit said, "Mitch, we met at the front door. And Leanna, you'll have your hands full with my little brother."

I whispered to Kit, "Stop telling stories. I won't be home for dinner, please tell CB I'm at the library studying."

"Why don't you tell her yourself, she's right behind you."

"Oh, hi Bridget. This is Leanna Johnson and she's my new girlfriend. We're going to her house for dinner, her folks are not home."

Mom didn't say a word to Leanna, she just stared at me and said, "You're going to be a priest for Gods sake's. A priest! And now you want to fool around with this girl? God will strike me down dead if you fool with the likes or her."

"Bridget, please wait until we leave before God strikes you down dead. It could be a real mess to clean up and Kit will want to do it by herself."

"Let's get out of here Leanna before God strikes her down. How does everyone like cooked Bridget? It would be quite a feast. Goodbye crazy Bridget." I laughed and grabbed Leanna's hand and lead her out the door.

Once we were out, Leanna said, "What was that all about.? Is she off mentally or what? She wouldn't even look at me. And she said, 'You want to fool around with this?' Does she hate every girl you go out with?"

"She thinks I'm going into the priesthood. I don't know what I'm going to do but keep one thing in mind, I like girls and I like you."

Once in Leanna's house she said, "Mitch, I'm a virgin. I don't know what you expected, but my bark is worse than my bite."

"I expected you to be a virgin and a very nice girl. Let's eat and laugh a little."

"Will you go to a party with me Saturday night? One of the girls I hardly know told me I could come if I could bring a boy. It's Donna from school that's having the party."

"Donna huh? Yes, I'd like to go with you. I can dance, but not very well. And, I'm sure you'll let me kiss you again, right?"

Leanna smiled and responded, "Kiss me? Yes, you can kiss me anytime you'd like. Now, for the important stuff; would you like Cheerios or Raisin Bran for dinner?"

"I thought you were going to make me dinner?"

"I am, Cheerios or Raisin Bran? I can't cook but I can make a mean bowl of cereal."

"I'll have Wheaties the breakfast of champions."

"You'll have Cheerios smart guy."

We both sat down and laughed and ate dinner and it was one of the best times I had since Syb broke up with me. The rest of this year could clearly be lots of fun with Leanne as my girlfriend.

GRADUATION & PRIESTHOOD

So, my new friend Leanna and I would become quite an item when we attended Donna's party Saturday night. I picked Leanna up at her house and met her folks and then we walked hand in hand to the party. Her parents were so nice. It was the kind of family I could only have wished to have had. Her dad was a cop and was not intimidating as I thought all cops were. I could see where Leanna got her good looks, it was from her mother. Her little sister and brother were really nice too.

When we arrived at the party all eyes were on Leanna and I. Donna walked to where we were standing by the end of the staircase and stuttered, "You… two … are together? You're… a couple?"

I said, "Yes, Leanna and I are together. Is there something wrong with that?"

Donna quickly got over her surprise and said, "I didn't think you two even knew one another. I guess stranger things have happened at good old OLPL."

Leanna was not going to pass up an opportunity to give Donna some grief, she replied, "Why Donna, you told me Mitch was your secret love and you'd do anything, including having sex with him to get him to love you. Or was it your best friend Judy that said that? Wait, now that I think about it, it was both of you that said that. I also remember it was only two days ago that you told me that."

Donna was stunned, she quietly said, "You can both leave my house, please do it right now."

I was really ticked off, but happy Leanna didn't back down. I said, "Donna, I know it's hard for you to accept new kids at our wonderful school, but you should remember you attend a Catholic school. And, as a Catholic, you should be kind and generous to all. If I were you, I'd ask God to forgive you for your sins here. Goodbye and good luck to you and your friends."

After Leanna and I got out of the house she laughed and said, "You are so much fun. Let's go to my house and play cards with my family."

I made a major decision in my short life; I would become a priest, or I would attempt to become a priest. I would continue seeing my good friend Leanna for the rest of the school year. Then I'd work in the summer at OLPL, doing maintenance work, mopping floors and lawn mowing. Because I was joining the seminary, my friend Sister Felicia, asked the powers to be, if I could work there this summer. I believe these jobs were offered only to people that were joining a religious order.

Needless to say, my mother CB, was overjoyed with my decision. She immediately took credit for my decision. She claimed it was her prayers that finally made God convince me to attempt to be a priest. Kit was quite angry with me. She wanted me to stay home and go to high school and then make the decision after that. I suppose she was right, but what the hell, I thought I might as well try it now. If I didn't like it, I could always come back and marry Leanna and have about a dozen kids. When I told her that she just laughed and said, "You better find a lot bigger woman than me, I'm not have a dozen kids even if it's God's wishes."

I kept asking Sister Felicia questions regarding the Catholic Church and the Catholic Bible. One of my main concerns was always about this celibacy thing and why women weren't allowed to be priests. Sister told me that the Catholic Church had issues with celibacy from the early days of the Christianity. She said, "Mitchell, according to our Catholic bible, the Apostle Peter took his believing wife along with him on his travels. Also, Matthew, Mark and John, told stories in their writings of Peter having a mother-in-law."

I replied, "So the old guys were married, that makes perfect sense. When they followed Jesus, he must have allowed them to stay married."

Sister said, "Mitchell, I should not tell you this, but it's along the same topic. There are other religions that believe Jesus was married to Mary Magdalene. Now, that's just what I've heard but it's not in the Catholic bible."

"Wow, I've never heard that before. But after you say that, it might make sense. From what I've read, that in the Jewish tradition, married life was professed to be more spiritual than that of the celibate life. Also, I've read that if a man at the age of thirty was not married he was consider different or odd. I'm not saying that Jesus was odd or different, but that is what I read."

Sister said, "You've done a lot research, more than most. I've never heard those assumptions, but the Church would not allow me to read such things. It seems to me that you'd be more comfortable in the religious life if you could marry."

"I have to admit, I like girls."

"There is nothing wrong with that. Let me try and explain what happened in the celibacy issue within the Church. Priests were allowed to be married and have sexual relations with their wives until approximately 1135 AD. There are several hypotheses of why there was this change. It has been argued that for many years that when a priest died his family would receive all his assets. The Church felt his assets belonged to the Church, thus the reason for wanting celibacy."

I shook my head and said, "It was all about money and wealth. Maybe by becoming a priest I can change the Vatican's thinking on all of this."

Sister smiled and replied, "Mitchell, you are such a good boy. I'm afraid you'll not change the thinking of an institution that's been around over two thousand years. I had the same ideas as a young woman entering the convent. I realized soon enough I wasn't going to change one thing. After that my goal was to teach children such as you about the Catholic Church the way I see it. Believe me when I say this, I am a very devout Catholic, but I do have my doubts, we all have.

As a young man entering the seminary, you also will have doubts. Ask questions and argue your point of view when you don't agree. Don't be disrespectful, always say you accept their teachings and wait to argue your point another day."

I was confused. Here was a member of a religious order giving me advice on arguing with the teachers at the seminary. She was also inferring that lots of what I'll hear is nothing but innuendos about other religions, fallacies and church doctrine. I was smiling when I replied, "Sister Felicia, you are the best teacher and best friend I could ever have imagined. You tell the truth when others continue to lie or spew something, they actually don't believe in. Thank you for all your help. I want you to know I'm not done picking your brain.'

Graduation finally came and all of us leftover OLPL students were happy to be moving onto our next venture in life. There was a graduation ceremony that was held in the school gym and Father Boyd did the officiating. This time he didn't ask any of the girls to sit on his lap as they received their diplomas. There was a party in the cafeteria and cake, coffee and soda pop were served. Leanna and her parents sat next to Kit, CB and me. Leanna held my hand to the astonishment of CB. CB whispered, "You're going to be a priest."

I replied, "Not today. Please let me enjoy this day without you grandstanding about your Catholic faith. If you keep this up, I'll be forced to tell everyone about you and the esteemed Father Bernard. How would you like that?" CB got up and said, "You don't know the truth about Father Bernard." She then upped and left the building and I assumed she walked home.

Leanne asked, "What did you say to her to have her leave?"

"Leanne, you don't want to know. I'm just glad she's gone so I can enjoy the moment with you, my sister Kit and your family."

Sister Felicia stopped by and said as she smiled and winked at me, "Mitchell, I had lots of fun with you this year. Please be good and do what they tell you to do at Nazareth Hall in the fall. And you Leanne, keep up the good work in your studies. I'd wager if you do, you'll someday be president."

SUMMER WITH CB

Kit and I returned home and found CB sulking in the living room. She was angry, angrier than I'd ever seen her in a long while. She screamed at Kit and me, "I don't appreciate you two ignoring me at the graduation party. And you Mitch, holding that little girl's hand. What goes through that mind of yours? Is nothing sacred to you? You've been picked by God Himself to represent Him here on earth and you're holding hands with a girl."

Kit smiled at me and said, "I can't wait to hear your response to this one."

I cleared my throat before saying, "Thanks Kit. And on to you crazy Bridget. It's none of your business, if and when, I hold someone's hand. And, by the way, didn't God pick you to represent Him here on earth too? But what did you do with that duty; you decided to sow your wild oats instead? So, after all that fun you had with all those unsavory men you screwed, you want me and Kit to do the duty God put you on earth to do. Well, crazy Bridget, it isn't going to happen this summer. Kit and I are going to do exactly what you did; we're going to screw our brains out and when there is nothing left of our brains like you, we may just go on a live a normal life."

CB just turned and walked away. Kit quietly said, "That went well."

I replied, "Yes, quite well. Do you think she'll shut up for a while now? I just can't stand that holier than thou crap."

Kit said, "Well you shut her up at least for today. You must remember she is mentally off."

I began my first day of work at OLPL and reported to Mr. Weaselly, who was the head janitor. He assigned me to yard duty. The work included mowing, trimming, raking and more mowing, raking and trimming. I was also told not to ask questions why, where or what. He told me point blank he was a no shit kind of guy and didn't like kids working for him. I felt right at home working for Mr. Weaselly. There were two other older men that worked only part-time. A guy named Bud, no last name given, and Larry Hallstad and elderly man of seventy-five. I liked Larry a lot. He was retired and wanted a job to get his mind off his wife's passing. Bud and Larry both worked inside the school and I was the outside man. When it rained, I worked inside with them.

After a few days of what I thought was hard labor, it rained, and I found myself inside with the older crew. Bud would not even acknowledge that I was alive. I was told by Larry that Bud had a bad drinking problem in his younger years and hated everyone. At lunch that day, I sat next to Larry and Bud in the school lunchroom. Larry asked where I would go to school next year, and I explained I was going into the priesthood and would begin my studies at Nazareth Hall in September. Bud started laughing immediately and said, "Yeah, another do-gooder. Why don't you go and get a job like all the rest of us had to do at your age? A priest? What kind of job is that? You think everyone will respect you and kiss your ass, don't you? Well, I for one have no respect for any damn priests."

Bud got up and walked away. Larry sat for a while before saying, "Just ignore him Mitch, he's had a hard life. He lost his wife at an early age to cancer. The priest at the only church in their little community, wouldn't allow the service to take place in his church, he said they were non-Catholic heathens. Evidently, he said some other derogatory things about his wife too. Bud and his wife frequented a tavern in the town.

When I say frequented, I mean every day. Everyone in town, including the priest knew about their social habits. He considered them lowlifes."

"Lowlifes? Because they frequented a tavern daily, he considered them lowlifes? Larry, I bet most folks have some kind of alcohol every day, I know my dad did."

Larry added, "It was a small town, a town where everyone knows what others are doing. Bud told me his wife was a teacher and a damn good one. The kids, other teachers, families and friends all loved her. She was not a drunk, but since they had no kids or other family members around the area, they socialized at the local tavern. She was a popular young woman and Bud believed the priest was jealous of anyone that was more popular than he was. Bud said he buried her on a friend's farm. They had the service there in a small area where the man had buried his wife and his parents. After her burial, Bud went to the priest's house and smacked the man in his face. He was arrested and was sent to the county jail for six months for assault. He had a previous record for drunk driving five years before, so he was sentenced to six months. Bud left that community right after he was released from jail. After that he just jumped from job to job, trying to forget the disgrace his dead wife endured at the hands of that priest."

I was flabbergasted by my friend Larry's comments, I replied, "Speaking of a lowlife, that priest was a lowlife. I don't understand how a priest or anyone else could do that to a person. Why in the world would the priest press charges against Bud, he had it coming?"

"I just don't know. Bud's a really good man once you get to know him. He's a hard man to get to know, however. It's taken me a long time to get to know him. I respect him very much. He was in the war and was wounded twice. He was a war hero."

"I don't know what I could ever say to make him feel any better about me and my plans. Larry, I have enough doubts about becoming a priest already and when I hear stories like this one, I wonder if I'm doing the right thing. One thing I'm sure of, I'd never do anything like what that priest did."

Larry smiled and said, "Mitch, please don't paint yourself with the same brush as that stupid priest, you're not like that. I think you'll make a fine priest and you'll make a difference. Most priests are good souls, there are a few that are not, but they are the exception to the rule."

A couple of weeks had passed when Bud stopped me out in the yard and said, "Mitch, you're a damn good worker. You work hard and do a real good job. You're not like the other kids we had here over the years. Keep up the good work. And, I'm sorry about what I said to you before about becoming a priest, if your work as a priest is as good as it is here, you'll make a very good priest."

I was surprised to say the least, I replied, "Thanks Bud, I hope I can do well, but who knows? Thanks for the nice comments about my work, it means a lot coming from you."

"Well I meant it. Take care, see you at lunch tomorrow."

I walked away very proud of myself. Here was a guy that didn't talk to me, didn't like me and hated the priesthood and I just may have won him over. Boy, I never felt so good. Maybe being a priest made a person feel like this all the time. I was beginning to think maybe I could make a difference.

I remained on the job until the first of September. Before I left for Nazareth Hall, Kit and I decided we would get Dad's old car running. The car was a 1956 Chevy Impala that sat in our garage since Dad's death over two years ago. I asked my new friends Bud and Larry if they could help us get it started. They both stopped by after work one day and looked the car over. Bud said, "Look, first we need to get a new battery and then check the gas in the tank. If its empty that's good, if not, we'll have a problem and we'll have to drain the tank."

Larry and Bud looked the whole car over and declared the car was in good shape. There was rust but they said that was to be expected. But the car engine had only thirty-three thousand miles on it, which they said was low mileage. The gas tank was empty, and we bought a new battery and also a can of gas. After installing the battery and putting a gallon of gas in the tank, it was time to try and start it. Bud turned the key and the car started immediately. The engine hummed and we backed it out of the garage. CB looked out the window and saw Dad's car backing out. She ran to the door and yelled, "What are you doing? I don't want you to take the car to the seminary, I want it here."

Kit yelled back, "Mom, it's for me, not Mitch. I'll need a car next year for college."

CB came out of the house and looked at my two friends, she said, "Who are these men?"

I introduced Bud and Larry to CB and they just stood and stared. I was wondering, 'Did they think she was good looking? Naw, they couldn't think that.'

But Bud said, "It's so nice to meet you Mrs. Collins, you have two fine children here. You should be very proud."

CB tried to straighten her hair with her hands and then smiled at Bud before saying, "Why thank you, yes they are very nice kids. Mitch is going to be a priest; did you know that?"

Bud replied, "Why yes I did. I've worked with your son all summer and I believe he'll make a damn good priest."

Larry quietly said, "Mrs. Collins, it was a pleasure meeting you, but Bud and I have to get on our way."

CB replied, "Don't you boys have time to come in and have a cup of coffee?"

Bud quickly said, "Yes, I have time even if Larry doesn't."

Larry and Bud walked into our house to the total dismay of Kit and me. I whispered to Kit, "What the hell is going on with CB. She's never let anyone into our house before. Do you think she in need of a man? Do you think she wants a sex partner?"

Kit turned and looked and me with a smile on her face, "Mitch, she's human. I never thought I'd ever say that again, but she's human, she needs a friend. She probably also needs to get laid, if you get what I mean?"

"Yeah, I think I get it, but CB, get real? She needs a friend?"

Kit added, "Mitch, everyone needs someone and CB needs someone now."

"Wow, you think she needs a companion, a male companion. Why can't she just find a woman to be her friend? What about our dad, he wanted her to be his companion, didn't he?"

"Mitch, shut up! This could be a nice thing for all of us. Let's just see what happens, they're just having coffee."

NAZARETH HALL

Kit and CB drove me to Nazareth Hall on Sunday morning just in time for ten o'clock mass. CB and Kit stayed until mass had ended and said their goodbyes. I was glad to have them leave when they did, it was tough on me seeing my sister Kit walk away. I was afraid for her, living alone with CB. Although Kit was a strong woman, CB could drive a person nuts.

I forgot to say that my former classmate little Jimmy Larson, had decided not to become a priest. He told me that personally while he was standing a half a block away. Leanna had told him about my conversation with Syb and he was afraid I'd beat the crap out of him for lying. I yelled at him, "You little shit, if I get close to you, I'll beat you to a pulp. You better apologize to Syb for lying about her." I faked running at him and he tore away. I never saw him close enough to confront him, it was probably for the best, I have to keep in mind I am going to be a priest.

Once in my dorm room, several of the guys I met during my summer stay, stopped by to say hello. I liked most of them, except Howard Dill. Howard was a braggadocio type of guy that thought the world revolved around him. He claimed to be quite a ladies man and a great athlete. He said he played football, basketball and baseball for his high school team in Elkwood. Elkwood was a town in a remote area of northern Minnesota. Most of us, or maybe all of us, had never heard of Elkwood and if we had, we would have known it was not a sports mammoth. I also wondered how large a school in that area really was.

I'm guessing the student body was about fifteen kids and half were girls. How could they even field a sports team? And, a ladies man with only seven or eight girls? OLPL had more girls than that.

After listening to fifteen minutes of Howard's bragging I asked, "How large a school is Elkwood?"

Howard replied, "How would I know? There were lots of kids, we drew from all the surrounding towns. I'm guessing about four or five hundred."

I laughed before saying, "Bull crap Howie! There are no schools in northern Minnesota that large. And, I bet you likely had around twenty kids in your class."

Howard defended his statements, "How would you know anything about our part of the state. You city kids think everyone else in this state are hicks. Well, we're not! We have great sports and lots of chicks and I was a big part of all of it. And, another thing, don't ever any of you clowns call me Howie ever again. It's Howard."

I laughed at him and replied, "Okay Howie, we won't call you Howard ever again."

Howie got up off the chair and walked out. The other three of us laughed at him.

A few days later, Howie was telling all the guys at our lunch table about his sexual exploits. I listened for quite a while and finally had enough, I said, "Howie, you're a big sex freak, aren't you?"

Howie smiled and replied, "You bet your ass I am."

"If that's your answer, I have a couple of questions of you?"

"That's my answer, what are your questions? I bet you want to know how many times I scored, don't ya? Well it's plenty."

I said, "No, I'd like to know if you went bare or with a skin?" I knew I had him, he didn't know what I was talking about. I could tell that neither did most of the other boys, but clearly Howie was the most confused.

He quickly said, "'With skin of course."

I replied, "What kind, ready-wet or dry and what brand?"

He didn't know I was asking about protection. He was more confused than before, he said, "What the hell are you talking about?"

A really big kid from the city of St. Paul by the name of Eric Randell said, "He's never had sex Mitch, he's all BS."

Howie had an angry look on his face like he was going to attack, he screamed, "I don't know what you two are talking about, I've screwed so many chicks and they all loved me?"

I said, "Are any of them carrying your babies?"

Again, Howie was confused, he replied, "Why are you asking that? No, I don't have any kids."

"Howie my simple-minded friend, don't you know that by having sex with a woman can produce children? Didn't Mommy and Daddy teach you about the birds and the bees?"

"What the hell are you talking about? Screwing is for fun not for having babies."

Eric laughingly said, "Young Howie here doesn't know where babies come from Mitch. Howie when you have sex with a woman, and not your hand, babies are what happens. When you use a skin, or commonly called a rubber, or a prophylactic, it's protection against getting the woman pregnant. Here in the big city we all know about those things. Maybe you should call Mom and Dad and ask them to tell you all about sex. And please, from now on, stop bragging about all the sex you've had, you have had none. And we now all know that."

Howie got up from the table as the whole lunchroom was laughing hysterically at him. He still didn't understand why we were laughing at him, but he figured he had made a mistake. A big mistake. He walked out of the lunchroom and headed for his next class. Eric and I just shook our heads and also left our seats. After we got out into the hall Eric said, "That guy is so full of it. I've listened to him for the last few days and I knew he'd never done it. What a blowhole." That was the end of Howie's bragging, he still was a bully, but I'll get into that later.

I found that Nazareth Hall's educational studies were not much different than any other school, except for philosophy and religion. The teachers were very good, I'd say the cream of the crop for Catholic studies. One priest, Father O'Neil was my homeroom teacher and also my religion teacher. He was a good guy and was also a fair-minded man to all the kids. He would answer all the questions that were thrown at him and no question was out of line. I realized that the question of celibacy that always entered my mind, was never questioned in this school. I figured that all these kids didn't care about that issue as much I did. I keep asking myself, maybe I'm not cut out to be a priest.

I asked Father O'Neil if I could meet with him after school one day, I had a question to ask of him. He agreed and we met in his office at four that afternoon. I began, "Father, I'm concerned that I'm not priest material. I have long running questions that I'd like your opinion about."

Father sat back in his chair and said, "Is your questions about celibacy and sex? If so, please realize that you are not the first to question these rules and you will not be the last. Now, ask away."

I sat for a minute realizing I was pretty embarrassed about this meeting. I hadn't realized most guys had the same questions. I began, "Father, sex is a pretty big thing for me. I really like girls and I have strong desires. I did have sex a couple of times and it was great. It was more than great, it was fantastic. So, what do I do?"

Father replied, "Mitchell, you are not alone. Reproducing is in your blood. Every man wants and needs to reproduce. The sex drive in young men is the strongest and you are experiencing that now in your life. You're attracted to women, but some are attracted to other men. But you must take control of that drive and not let it control you. If you can't control it, the priesthood is not going to be for you. I have this conversation every single day, in fact you are the third person today that came to me. Our dropout rate is higher than anyone would expect. That's good, not everyone is cut out to be a priest."

I sat back in my chair and said, "So, the dropout rate is high, and you expect that? I thought it would be low but the more I think about it, other guys I'm sure have these questions."

"The worst thing that happens is that our young men are afraid to drop out because it will disappoint family or friends. Some stay here for a long time just not to disappoint anyone, which is so wrong. Anyone that does such a thing will make a very poor priest. Some of the bad things you hear about priests doing is because of the social pressures put on you young men. This place is designed to train young men for the priesthood, but also to weed out the ones that should not be priests. Does that make sense?"

"It does Father. I was raised by a mother that told me from the time I was an infant, that I was going to become a priest. Well, I do have my doubts. I'm glad I'm not alone and I hope God directs me in the right direction."

Father added, "He will, He will."

FIRST YEAR

One night I just couldn't sleep. We were in the midst of first semester finals and I thought a slow walk around the building would help. I walked outside to a very cold December evening without a coat. I knew this would be a short walk. Just before I turned the corner of the building, I heard someone saying, "Listen you little shit, you'll give me the answers to that history test tomorrow. Write them down as soon as you get out of the class and give them to me at lunch. If you don't, I'll kick the shit out ya. Do you understand? Now, get the hell away from me."

It was little Davy Pearson, the smallest kid in our class and he was being told to cheat by a bully. Davy almost ran into me as he ran around the corner crying his eyes out. I grabbed a hold of him and said, "Davy, go back to your room and don't you ever help this fool out again. I'll take care of him."

Howie walked around the corner to face me. He said, "This is none of your business Collins, this is between Davy and me"

I smiled at hayseed Howie and replied, "Listen hayseed, I'm making it my business. This will be the last kid you ever torment in this school. Davy will not cheat for you, nor will anyone else. If it's a fight you want, I'll give it to you. Either way you'll lose. I'm going to tell Father O'Neil about what you're doing to Davy and all the other little kids you've been bullying. That crap is over with tonight. Do you understand?"

Howie hauled off and smacked me in the nose. Blood flew out of my nose and all over Howie. Howie saw the blood and my nose flatten on my face and he turned and ran away. Even though I was bleeding like a stuffed pig, I ran after him. He was about five yards away from me when he turned to see if I was still following him. He tripped and fell flat on his face. He was crying like the big baby that he was, but it didn't matter to me. I jumped on top of him and turned him over, so he was facing me. I then began to pummel his face with both my fists. He attempted in vain to stop me, but I just pushed his hands away. I must have hit him ten to fifteen times when someone yanked me off of him. It was Father Madison and he was pissed.

Father Madison was a no crap kind of guy and he was also a mean-spirited priest. He yelled at me, "Get back into the dorm and wait in your room until I come to see you." I then heard him say, "Howard, you poor boy, I'm so sorry this happened to you. Mitchell Collins will be sorry for what he has done to you and will wish he was never born, after I get through with him. Come on son, let me help you."

I walked back to my room holding a handkerchief to my nose to try and stop the bleeding. As I entered my room, my roommate Eric Randell said, "What's all the noise out there? Is there a fire drill?" Eric then looked at my face and was shocked at what he saw, he said, "What in the world happened to you?"

I quickly said, "That hayseed Howie sucker punched me. I heard him tell little Davy Pearson to give him the answers to a history test or he'd beat him up. I told him I'd tell Father O'Neil about what he was doing, and he slugged me. He then ran away. After I realized what he did to me, I chased him down and caught him. I then beat the crap out of him. Father Madison pulled me off of him and took Howie's side. He said he'd see me after he attended to that hick Howie."

Eric said, "Get your butt out of here and go and tell Father O'Neil what happened. He'll sort it out without judging you first."

I replied, "Good plan." I got up and walked towards the priest's residence. Before I got to the door Father Madison came walking out.

Madison asked, "What are you doing here, I told you to wait in your room?"

I replied, "I'm here to speak to Father O'Neil, not you."

Madison said, "You'll speak to me and only me, do you understand?"

"No! I don't understand. That jerk Howie cold cocked me."

"Did it occur to you, that maybe he had a reason to do so? Just maybe, he was threatened by you and figured he best be physical with you before you harmed him. He's afraid of you and he has reason to be. You're a big boy and clearly you have a bad temper. You started this and I will end it. I'm going to suggest to our principal Father Rowen that you be expelled from our esteemed school."

I was getting more and more pissed off at this holier than thou priest, I yelled, "Maybe, if you looked into both sides of the whole episode, you'd find out you're wrong! I just don't care any longer if I get kicked out of here, but if you do that, you'd better kick that hayseed Howie out too."

"You are so out of line here. I suggest you shut that big mouth of yours before I shut it for you."

A moment later Father O'Neil walked out of the rectory and asked, "What in the world is going on out here? Mitchell are you alright? Who beat you? Have you been seen by a doctor?"

Father Madison interjected, "No, he hasn't! But he did beat a defenseless boy to a pulp. That poor Howard may need stitches to close his wounds."

Father O'Neil replied, "I would never believe that Mitchell here would beat someone up without provocation. Did you Mitchell?"

I said, "No Father, I didn't. Howie was forcing little Davy Pearson to give him the answers to the history test tomorrow. He's been picking on all the little kids, Davy in particular, since school began. I just put an end to it. Just ask Davy. Madison here refused to listen to me, he took Howie's side immediately. And by the way, Howie hit me first, he sucker punched me and ran away, but I caught him."

Father Madison quickly replied, "First off, my name is Father Madison to you. Secondly, I don't believe one word you're saying."

Father O'Neil quietly said, "Let's all go and talk to Davy. Please let me do the talking, you two are not in the right frame of mind to ask any pertinent questions."

We walked into the rectory and Father O'Neil called and asked the dorm counselor to please have Davy come to the rectory. Davy knocked at Father O'Neil's office door and he stepped in. Father quietly said, "Davy please sit down, I have a couple of questions of you."

Davy sat down and looked at me and said, "I'm so sorry Mitch. That Howie's a real jerk. He shouldn't have hit you."

Father said, "That's what were here to determine Davy. Did Howard strike Mitchell first?"

Davy's eyes were wide open when he said, "Did he? You bet he did! Mitch was just helping me out. He told Howie that he was going to report him for making me cheat for him. He also told him that he was done picking on us little kids."

Father O'Neil looked at Father Madison and said, "Well, this is quite a different story than you've heard from Howard, isn't it?"

"I for one believe Howard. You didn't see this animal on top of that young defenseless boy, getting beat to a pulp. If I hadn't shown up, poor Howard might have died from his injuries. This boy should be expelled from our institution. What kind of example does this set for all of our fine boys that want to become priests?"

Father O'Neil said in return, "Father we have a difference of opinion here, so I suggest we have Principal Rowen settle this."

We were told to return to our rooms, and we'd be called to meet in the morning. Davy shook his head and said, "Mitch, I'm sorry about this, but that Howie is a real dirt bag. He has picked on me from the first day I came here. He started on me right after I laughed about him not knowing how babies were made."

"Davy just tell the truth tomorrow. I really don't care if they kick me out. If they are going to allow guys like Howie to get away with that crap, I don't want to be a part of this."

The next morning Davy was asked to report to the principal's office. He spent the better part of an hour with both priests and the principal. When the meeting was over Father Rowen said to Davy, "Go back to your classes and do not talk to anyone about what was discussed here today. You are in no trouble."

Davy walked into class and said nothing. I realized that none of the other students knew what had happened last night. They all saw the doctor come into the building but didn't know why. My roommate Eric just told everyone I fell out of bed. I have no idea what Howie told them; I'm guessing nothing. Later in the day after classes were done, I got a message to go to the principal's office. I walked in and Father Rowen was sitting with Father O'Neil. Rowen spoke, "I guess you'd like to know what your future holds. To begin with, beating another student up will not be tolerated here at Nazareth Hall. In both cases, either one of you could have killed the other person. So, for that, you will both be on probation. If you get into another altercation you will be expelled. For the next two weeks, after classes are completed for the day, you will both be confined to your dorm rooms. Food will be brought to your rooms. Do you have anything to say?"

I nodded my head no. After that, Father said, "There are some things I think you should know about Howard and the reason we're being lenient with him. He's come from a weird family life where he and his mother lived in a one-bedroom house in the back of her parent's property. His father left the family as soon as Howard was born. Howard was home schooled and didn't have any friends. His whole life was his mother. He doesn't know how to communicate very well with others and his education leaves a lot to be desired. He's what we here at Nazareth Hall call socially inept. We will be working with him on his skills of dealing with others. He's to stay away from the smaller kids and no fighting. I explained to him the little kids he's picking on now will likely be much bigger than him in a year or so. And, if he's not careful they'll be after him."

I just sat still and said nothing. I couldn't believe what I was hearing. They were blaming me for the whole thing. I'm sitting here with a broken nose and it's my fault. Poor Howie was brought up in a shitty home life. What about me? I was too, but I didn't pick on the little kids. I looked at Father O'Neil, but he wouldn't make eye contact with me. I felt betrayed, not just by O'Neil but by this whole group of priests. I didn't know what I'd do, but I was not going to take this lying down. I'd let them all know how I felt.

I walked back to my dorm room and sat at my desk. Eric said, "You look pissed off and very unhappy. Did they blame you and not the hick?"

"Yeah, it was all my fault. The hick was brought up by his mom in a one-bedroom house. She home schooled him. No wonder he didn't know about having babies. They said something like 'he's socially inept.' I think that means he doesn't know how to talk to people. How in the hell is he going to be a priest if he can't talk to people? I'd bet a hundred bucks he doesn't last two years. He's so stupid he's flunking all of his classes. So much for home schooling. I've been put on probation and can't leave this room unless it's to go to classes. I must eat my meals in here. I hope I can use the bathroom, they never mentioned that."

I spent my prison time in my room reading the Catholic bible. I didn't find anything in it to make me feel better. In it, God said I was to turn the other cheek. I couldn't do that since hayseed Howie broke my nose square in the middle of my face. I don't know how anyone could say hit me again after someone broke their nose. Maybe I'm not priest material.

Late one afternoon Father O'Neil rapped on my prison door and said, "Mitchell, may I come in, it's Father O'Neil?"

I replied, "Yeah, open the bars and come on through."

Father smiled as he entered the room and said, "How are you doing? You must be getting lonesome in here all night."

I responded, "No, it's nice being alone to ponder my future. I'm getting to the point in my life that I think the priesthood is different than I expected. Now I can see you priests are worried sick about hayseed Howie, but what about Davy and me? Don't we count? Hayseed was the aggressor and he is also a bully. But what did you priests say about him; 'he's socially inept.'"

Father retorted, "Mitchell, you have to understand a few things here. First, we cannot allow violence of any kind here. Second, we are dealing with a boy that has social issues that we're trying to deal with. It would be unfair if we didn't treat Howard a bit different than the rest of you normal boys. Thirdly, and lastly, we are Christians, and we must help the oppressed and downtrodden. Clearly Howard has been oppressed and downtrodden all of his life."

I just sat there and shook my head, I finally laughingly said, "What about my home life. No one has ever asked me what I came from. I guarantee it was as bad as poor little Howie's was or maybe worse. I was raised by a crazy mother that told me in no uncertain terms I was going to be priest. She began that crap when I was three. My sister was forced to go into a convent. She finally said, 'I quit,' and left. My father lived in our basement until he died, and I hardly knew him. You know Father O'Neil; I hate people that assume we all had the wonderful lives you priests had. Well many of us didn't."

"I'm sorry you feel that way Mitchell. I'm sure our principal didn't mean to offend you or anyone else. I'm sure he knew nothing of your family life. I'll say this to you, buck up and work hard and get through this year before you decide to quit. Have a good evening."

I stayed at the Hall for the reminder of the year. I only spoke to Father O'Neil when I had to. I never asked him another question about the church or the bible. I also never spoke another word to Father Madison or to Father Rowen. In addition, I never uttered another word to hillbilly Howie, since he was off limits to me. I watched him from afar and he was still picking on the smaller kids but not quite as violent as he had before.

THE TRUTH

I had the option of staying on at Nazareth Hall that summer, but I chose to go home. I wanted to see my sister Kit and spend some quality time with her. When I got home, however, I found out Kit had a boyfriend. Now, having a boyfriend was a new thing for Kit and she was the happiest that I'd ever seen her. She was laughing and giggling all the time. I finally asked her, "Am I ever going to meet Mr. Perfect."

Kit said to me, "Mickey and I are going out to a party this afternoon and you can meet him when he picks me up. Oh Mitch, he's so cute, so nice to me and so much fun. I know you'll like him."

I replied, "Does CB know about Mr. Wonderful?"

"Yes, she does, and she likes him."

"CB actually said she likes him. I don't believe it. Is she drinking or on drugs? Come on Kit, she doesn't like anyone that isn't wearing a priest's cassock, with a white collar."

"Mitch, she's changed since she met Bud and Larry. The three of them have become great friends. They all go to church together on Sundays and come back here and she makes them breakfast. They've become sort of our family. They're both here a lot."

I just stared at her before saying, "What are you saying, my two old friends are now courting CB?"

"I wouldn't say courting, but the three of them have fun together. They laugh all the time and she is so nice to the both of them."

"You do know that Larry is in his seventies?"

"Yes, I do and so does Mom. Mitch, it's not about love and sex, it's about friendship. And if it did end up in love or in sex, what do you care? She's happy for the first time in a long while, and I'm happy for her. And Mitch, I'm happy too. I know I'm young and I just met Mickey a few months ago but I'm crazy about him. Just maybe I've found the man of my dreams."

"This is a lot to take in. I'm happy you've met someone, but be careful, you have college in the fall, and I don't want you pregnant."

"Having a baby is not going to happen to me, at least not for now. Mickey is going to barber college right now and when he's done, he'll go to work with his dad who owns a barber shop."

"Kit in a very short time your life has changed. I'm glad you're happy but I still worry about you. And CB, that is a real story. By the way, where is she?"

"She and the boys are out to lunch. They do this all the time. Now, I don't want you to get mad or upset with what I'm going to tell you, but Mom has offered our basement to the boys to live in. Part of the agreement is that they will have to finish it into an apartment with two bedrooms and a closed in bathroom. There will be a small kitchen in front too. They plan on starting work next week."

"Kit why are you calling them boys. They're old men for God's sake. I'm really confused. Is this why you two never came to see me after you dropped me off? I've had lots of trouble at the Hall and no family to talk to. Did you both forget me for those other men? I feel like I'm all alone. If I had known all this, I would have spent the summer at the Hall."

Kit had tears running down her cheeks, she quietly said, "You needed us? You had lots of trouble? Oh Mitch, I'm so sorry. We just thought everything was going so well. We had no idea. Tell me what happened."

I stood up and was walking away when I said, "Screw you. You're turning out to be just like your mother, very self-centered and the only person and thing you care about is yourself. Leave me alone, please."

As I walked away, I could hear Kit crying out loud and that stung me. I love my sister like I'd love a mother, only one that cared about me. So, I turned around and said, "Listen Kit, I'm sorry, it's just difficult for me hearing about all this happiness you and CB are having and I'm having none. I'll be happy to meet your Mickey Mouse this afternoon." I joked, "His name is Mickey Mouse, isn't it?"

Through her tears I saw a smile, she ran and jumped into my arms and squeezed me. Kit was now laughing hysterically and said, "I like it, Mickey Mouse. He'd be so mad if he heard me calling him that. Oh Mitch, I love you so much, please don't ever get mad at me again and please for my sake give Mom a second chance."

"You always make it hard for me to stay mad at you. But CB, come on? She's ruined my life and now she's found happiness in the arms of two old farts that were my friends. Now they all want to live here in my dad's house. You can understand why I'm not happy, can't you?"

"Please give them a chance and please be nice to Mickey Mouse, he'll be here in an hour." Kit left me alone so she could get all dressed up for the now infamous Mickey Mouse. I realized I didn't even know his last name or if he had one or not.

There was knock on the door and I looked out and saw Kit's new boyfriend standing there. I opened the door and asked, "Where are the flowers and the candy you cheap shit."

Mickey laughed and replied, "I'm broke, I'm just a struggling college kid. A barber college kid at that."

"Come on in Mickey, I'm Mitch, Kit's long-lost brother home for the summer."

"Nice to meet you Mitch, Kit talks about you all the time. If you were not her brother, I'd be jealous. Please call me Mike instead of Mickey. My folks have always called me Mickey and I hate it. I let Kit call me that because she said she loves that name. My last name is Gorman."

"Mike Gorman it is then. Did you just start barber school?"

"Yeah, it's just a one-year course, I'll be done next summer. Is Kit here?"

"Yes, I'll get her." I yelled, "Kit Collins, get your butt out here, Mike is here and stop calling him Mickey Mouse. He hates that name. I did that for you Mike."

Kit came running out of her bedroom and said, "You don't like the name Mickey? I thought you said your whole family called you that?"

Mike quietly said, "I'm sorry Kit, but I thought you liked it, but I don't. It would be like calling you Kitty."

"Oh, I see, I'd hate being called Kitty. Let's get out of here and party. Mitch, good luck with Mom, they just pulled up out front."

Kit and Mike walked out the front door as CB, Bud and Larry were walking in. They all met on the front steps and it was like old home week for all of them. I stayed inside and watched them all from the bay window in our living room. Hugs and smiles all around and all I could think of was I was just an outsider. After Kit and Mike walked away the new three amigos walked in.

After CB entered the house, she saw me and ran to give me a hug. I backed away and said, "Please, don't do that crap to me. I don't need your hugs or your affection."

Bud walked over to me and said, "Please be nice to your mom, she loves you. And, how are you?"

I looked Bud over and said, "What in the hell are you two doing here with Bridget? Are you trying to score with this old whore here?"

Larry stepped in front of Bud and quietly said, "Please, be polite. We mean your mother no harm. We're all just friends. Great friends, I might add!"

I smiled and said, "Well thanks for that Larry, I so happy you two are courting Bridget and are preparing to live here with her. My dad would be so happy you two are moving into his house. And you Bridget, moving these two into my dad's house? I'm going back to the Hall today; I've got to get away from you."

Bud stepped in front of me and quietly said, "Mitch, please come with me to the backyard, I want to talk to you about somethings you don't know."

Larry added, "I think I better come along too. Bridget, please wait in the house for us. Thanks, my dear, it shouldn't take us too long."

I followed the boys, yes, I said boys. I was not happy about this at all. The guts these two old farts had wanting to talk to me about my dear Mom. There were three lawn chairs sitting in the backyard and I then realized they had prepared this all for me. It was a set up, but I'd hear what they had to say.

Bud was the first to speak, he began, "First off I need to tell you my real name; it's Patrick Fitzpatrick. Of course, having that name led to people always joking about my name, so I just called myself Bud. Mitch, I met your dad after I got out of the service. I was wounded in the war. Well it was more than once, and the last time it was bad enough to get discharged. I was drinking pretty hard in those days; it was before I met my wife. I was introduced to your dad at a bar called the Cedar Inn. Your pa was about four years older than me and was also a very heavy drinker. When we were drinking pretty hard, he would always start bragging." Bud stopped for a minute and asked if he could get a glass of water. I was getting interested in what he was saying so I ran and got him the water.

Bud swallowed some of the water and continued, "As I was saying, your pa like to brag. He told me the story about how he met your ma. It was down at Hiawatha lake one summer where all the young high school girls congregated to meet boys and swim. They all wore those cute little swimsuits, but not as reviling as today's swimsuits. He spotted her right off and went after her. She was going into eleventh grade the next year and was just sixteen or seventeen years old. Your pa was at least twenty-two or twenty-three at the time. He said he told her he was eighteen and he wanted to take her out on a date. She liked him right off and thought he was a very handsome fella. They began to secretly date one another, and it led to them having sex. Your mom was a virgin and your dad wasn't very experienced either, he was likely a virgin too. He never would say that, however."

Bud stood up and walked around his chair a couple of times. He said, "My legs hurt if I sit too long. You know, from my war injury. Well, your mom got pregnant with your dad's baby. He said if she told her folks or anyone else, he'd go to jail for statutory rape, meaning having sex with minor. He had to finally admit to her he was twenty-three years old. So, your mom would never tell her parents or any of her friends it was your daddy Frank's baby. She dropped out of school when she began to show. She had the baby girl four months later at general hospital. She gave that baby away for adoption."

Larry finally said something, "Do you understand all of this so far Mitch" Your dad always told everyone that would listen to his BS, that your mom was having sex with all kinds of guys in high school. When in fact, she was only having sex with a man that was six or seven years older than her."

I sat there mesmerized by what I was hearing. I quietly said, "So, it was my dad's baby, not some stranger? Is there more to this story?"

Bud replied, "I'm just getting started. After your mom got rid of the evidence of your father's indiscretion, he went full steam ahead with the booze and other women. Your mom was living at home in disgrace, with no friends and a family that wouldn't talk to her. About a year after the baby was given up, your mom ran into Frank at the same lake where she met him. He was drunk and he had the guts to walk up to her and tell her how much he loved her. He was so sorry for what he had done to her and wanted to make it right. He asked her to move into the new house he had just bought and become a couple. Your mom was still a very naive young girl of eighteen. Since she had no friends or family, she jumped at the chance to be with the man she loved. After a few weeks, Frank began to get home late at night and was always drunk. I saw him around in those days and I always asked him what he was doing. I used to say to him, you have that lovely young lady at home, why are you always whoring around? He would always say, 'Bud you wouldn't understand. It's in my blood. I need a different woman every night and that little Bridget is not taking care of my needs.'

Again, Bud got up and walked around the chair before starting again, "A year or so after that conversation I had with him, he told me Bridget was pregnant again. He said she wasn't satisfying him when using a condom, so he wouldn't wear one. He said to me and this is no lie, 'If she gets pregnant again, she'll have to have it removed.' I asked him what he meant by 'removed' and he said, 'cut it out.' I said, you mean an abortion. He smiled and replied, 'Yeah, that's exactly what I mean. That dumb bitch better figure out how not to get pregnant when I'm screwing her because I'm not wearing a rubber ever again.' Well, needless to say, she got pregnant. At that time there were no birth control pills available to young single girls. Bridget had no choice to do what Frank said. She had no family to go home to and she was a disgrace in the neighborhood. It was taboo to get pregnant in high school and that stigma would stay with her the rest of her life."

Again, Bud stood up and walked around his chair. After he sat down, he began again, "I hope I'm not upsetting you too much Mitch, but you need to hear all of this."

I replied, "I'm okay, with hearing all of this, I think I have misjudged my mom all these years."

Bud said, "Alright then, I'll continue. Your dad wanted your mom to abort the baby or give it for adoption, but she refused, and Kit was born. She was healthy baby and your dad left your mom and Kit alone for at least three months. She had to go to the Catholic church and beg for food for herself, pablum and milk for the baby. Father Bernard was the priest that helped her out and he personally paid for all her needs. He did not, however, have anything sexual to do with your mother. I'll get to that later. Your dad finally came home and told your mom point blank; she better not have any more kids. He wasn't going to support anymore of her kids. She said to him, 'Then no more sex.' His reply was, 'Where the hell do you think I've been for the last three months? My friend Judy Schubert takes good care of me. But you will still cooperate if you want to live here. When I want it, you'll give it to me!' I'm quoting this from conversations I actually had with your dad. These are the things he said he had told your mom. Your mom will verify everything I've said."

I replied, "What about me? Was he happy I was born?"

Bud laughed, he said, "Happy you were born? No! He was not. In fact, he wanted you aborted or given up for adoption too. Your mom refused. When you were born your mom kicked him out of the house for several months. He returned but lived downstairs and she wouldn't allow him into her bedroom or to see you kids. She said if he tried, she'd go to the police and tell them he raped her when she was sixteen. He stayed away from her bedroom after that."

Bud stretched his arms and continued, "Now, about Father Bernard. Your mom was going to bible study at the rectory at OLPL twice a week with several other women. You always had a babysitter when she left you and your sister. That night your father followed her and saw she went into the rectory. He thought she was having sex with the priest. He barged into a conference room in the basement and found the priest and five women sitting around a table with their bibles open. He was drunk as usual and started screaming at the priest that he was having sex with his wife. He attacked Father Bernard and beat him to a pulp. After that he went to see the bishop and told him he wanted that sexual deviate Father Bernard removed from the parish. If he didn't, he'd sue the church. The bishop told him if he stayed away from the church and school, Father would not press charges. Later, Father asked for a transfer and it was granted. There was a woman named Helen Anderson that was in the bible study class with your mom. If you'd like she will collaborate what I just told you."

I replied, "There is no need for that Bud, I believe everything you've said."

"One last thing. Judy Schubert isn't any saint. If anything, she was the neighborhood whore. She did have your dad live at her place from time to time. However, she was a professional. What I mean is she is a prostitute. Maybe not so much now that she's older. But when she was young, she was very active. I know the BS story about Frank beating up her husband, I heard it plenty of times. The truth is, she was never married. It was her pimp your old man beat up. The reason was, he owed the pimp some money and refused to pay. After he beat up the pimp, he was almost beaten to death by the pimp's bodyguards. Some folks around town believe that was the reason for his early demise. Your mother is a good woman. The reason she told your sister she was going to become a nun was to keep your old man away from her. He wanted her and wanted her badly. When I say wanted, I mean he wanted her in his bed. That's why your mom insisted on her trying the convent. It was a way to get her out of the house and away from Frank. As for you, she just wanted to get you away from him. She admits she went overboard on the religion. But she was so remorseful for what she had done as a high school kid, it was her only way of getting by."

"You've got to be kidding me," I quietly said. "That poor woman went through all that crap for Kit and me. I've treated so poorly. She always said I didn't know the whole truth and I didn't. I've got a lot of apologizing to do. I assume you've told Kit this whole story. She had really changed about Mom."

"Your sister got the same lecture from Larry and I a while ago. I just couldn't stand seeing you guys treating your mom so poorly when you didn't know the whole story. I also want you to know I love your mother and I want to marry her, if she'll have me. Larry told me he explained my wife's death to you. I been by myself for a very long time and I want to share the rest of my life with Bridget."

As I stood up, I said, "Bud, I hope she says yes, you're a pretty good guy. And Larry, you are too. I've got to go see my mother, thanks guys."

MAKING AMENDS

I walked in the backdoor of the house and there sitting in a kitchen chair was my mom. I said, "I've just had my eyes opened by Bud and Larry. They explained everything about Frank. It appears he lied to me and to Kit about you and your background. In fact, he was the real loser around here. I can't ever tell you how sorry I am that I treated you the way I did. That stuff he told us about that priest Father Bernard, was so bad and I believed him. I couldn't imagine why you wanted me to be a priest after I heard that story. I promise things will be different from now on. I hope you can forgive me."

Mom got up and walked over to me and hugged me hard and cried. After we were still in our embrace she said, "Mitchell, I love you so much. There was never anything you said that would ever stop me from loving you. The only question I have now is, are you going to stay with us this summer?"

"I'm staying."

"Thank God for that."

Kit returned home several hours later and knocked on my bedroom door. I opened it and Kit shyly said, "Can I come in?"

"Yeah, you can, but thanks for setting me up, by the way. I guess that was the best way however, I needed something to wake me up to what really happened around here."

Kit smiled, hugged me and cried. We held each other for a long time before she choked out the words, "We were so wrong about Mom.

It wasn't her; it was him all along. I've been crying for weeks over this. Larry and Bud told me everything. Our wonderful father wanted to have sex with me. Mitch, I would have killed him before I'd have let that happen, or he'd have killed me."

"I would have killed him too if he had tried anything on you. That bastard!"

"Mom is so happy we finally found out the truth. She knew we'd never believe her. Can you believe our grandparents disowned her? She lived in grief with having to give up her baby. And then, that awful man treated her like a sex object and a sex slave. Mitch, we owe her a debt of gratitude for protecting us. We also must treat her as our mother and not a crazy lady."

"I agree and I already told her that. Now, on another topic, are you and Mike, or Mickey, getting hitched soon? If so, I'd like to be home when that happens. I really liked Mike and you have my blessings to marry him."

"Slow down little brother. I like him. I like him a lot. But getting married will be at least a year away, or maybe more depending on my school and him. If he continues treating me like he does, I'd have a hard time letting him get away. Mitch, he is so nice to me. I also seen how he treats his mother and his sisters. He so nice to all of them. His dad left the family years ago and remarried. Mike has a good relationship with his dad, but the rest of the family does not. When he finishes barber school he'll work with his dad, but it will take a while to get a customer base. That's why, if we remain in love, I'll need to get my nursing degree."

"I distinctly heard you say, 'remain in love,' are you in love with him?"

"Mitch, I just don't know. I don't know what love is all about. I do know that when I'm with him I'm so happy and when I'm not with him I'm not happy. So, I guess that's love."

"Good for you. I felt that way with Sybil, but I was just too young for love. Oh Kit, what is going to happen to me? I just don't know where I belong. I had some issues at the Hall this year and I gave myself another year. If things don't get better, I'll leave. Some of these priests are pretty bad. One in particular I thought was a good guy, but he didn't back me up when a problem arose, and I was disciplined. I was only defending a little kid that this jerk was bullying. I'm sorry about having to tell you my sad little story, but I needed to get that off my chest."

Kit sat very stoic and had listened to my tale of woe without blinking an eye. She replied, "Whatever you decide will be alright with me. I really appreciate you being able to tell me these personal things, it makes me feel closer to you."

"Kit you made up for not having a mother most of my life. I love you so much and I feel I can tell you anything and you'll never judge me poorly."

"Thanks, that's the way I feel too. Remember I didn't have a father, you took his place. I love you too."

The boys, Bud and Larry, began working on the basement apartment the following Monday. Larry had quit his job at OLPL, and Bud was now the head of all maintenance. Mr. Weaselly had retired, and Bud took over. He worked about nine hours a day and came to the house and worked another five of six hours on the basement. Larry worked all day but couldn't do all of the things by himself. I worked alongside Bud at OLPL and I was having the time of my life with him. He was such a good man and was very funny. When I got home, I also helped the boys. Soon Mom, Kit and Mike Gorman were all helping out at night. It was like having a family working together. Bud was in charge and he would instruct everyone on what to do. Larry was next in charge. There were times when we were all laughing so hard, we couldn't stop.

I could see the love Kit and Mike had for one another. They were so happy. It reminded me of Syb and I after we had sex the second time. We were so in love. I always wondered how she was and if she had a boyfriend. It drove me craze thinking of her kissing another guy and having sex with him. I was praying I'd see her this summer and right away God answered my prayer.

I was walking home from work one afternoon when Syb came out of her house and yelled, "Hey handsome, got time to say hello?"

I quickly stopped and walked towards her house. She didn't make eye contact with me, she appeared to be looking at her shoes. She lifted her head a bit and smiled and sheepishly said, "It so nice to see you. I've seen you walk by, but I was afraid to say hello. I thought you'd be mad at me."

I was stunned by her comment, I replied, "Mad at you? Never! I missed you so much and I was hoping to see you this summer. You look great, is everything okay?"

"Yes, everything is fine. I missed you too, probably more than you'll ever know."

"Do you have a main squeeze, I bet you do? Anyone that looks likes you will have all the guys falling at your feet."

"I did have a guy that I kind of liked. But as you know, I'm not having sex again unless I'm married. He didn't like that, and he dumped me. Good riddance I'd say."

I was happy she got dumped, it might lead to a romance for me this summer. I happily asked, "How about you and I go to a movie tonight."

Syb shook her head no and replied, "No Mitch, you're going to be a priest and I don't want to screw that up for you. I think we should remain friends."

I thought, 'What a bummer!' I then smiled and said, "Well thanks for at least saying hello. Take care and have a great summer." I slowly walked away hoping she'd say, 'Wait a minute big guy, I love you.' It didn't happen and I jogged quickly to my house.

After changing my clothes, I was going downstairs to help the boys out when my mom shouted, "Mitch, you have a visitor."

I turned around and walked into the living room and there was Syb standing in the doorway. She asked, "Is the invitation to go to a movie still an option?"

I said, "Why yes, it is. But first off, I'd like to introduce you to some new family members."

Syb looked confused. Very confused! She asked, "Family? I know your family."

I grinned and said, "Follow me down to our basement. Everyone is working down there so I may have to stay here awhile."

After Syb and I got downstairs Kit ran right over and said, "Syb, it's so nice seeing you. I hope you're here to spend time with my brother. He needs a friend."

I quickly said, "Kit, what's that all about. I have friends."

Syb smiled at Kit and said, "Yes he needs a female in his life. Well at least for the summer. You know playing with boys all year is not fun."

I then began the introductions, "This is my friend Sybil Newman, these are our new family members, Bud Fitzpatrick, Larry Hallstad and Kit's friend Mike Gorman."

Syb said, "It nice to meet all of you but I do know Mike a little bit from school."

Mike smiled at Kit and replied, "Kit, I asked Sybil out to a school dance once and she turned me down. She was going with someone at the time and I was just chopped liver to her."

Syb raised her voice and said, "I never said that you were chopped liver, whatever that means."

Mike was laughing hard he sputtered the words, "Just… kidding, just… kidding."

Kit stepped in and replied, "You two guys leave Syb alone, do you hear me? And you Mickey Gorman, we're going to pick up the pizzas. After we all eat, we have work to do."

Syb grabbed my hand and said, "Would you walk me home, I want to change clothes. I'm working with you guys too."

Syb and I walked hand in hand to her house and I sat in the living room while she changed. I did ask her if I could watch her change, but she just gave me a disgusted look. I said, "What? It's not like I haven't seen you get dressed before." Again, a looked of disgust, followed by a big smile, as she pulled the front of her sweater up to her head. She did have on her bra, but it was fun watching her just the same. She laughed and laughed.

We went back to our house and had pizza with my new family and then we all worked on the basement. We all laughed, and it was such a fun time. Kit announced that it was the first time that she and I ever had a family party and we both loved it. Syb stayed until one o'clock and then I walked her home. When we got to her house she said, "Do you want to see more of me this summer, or should I disappear?"

I said, "You better not disappear after I saw you in your bra. Why would you ask a question like that? I want to spend as much time as I can with you. I think you forget, I'm still in love with you."

"Mitchell Collins, I'm still in love with you too, but you're going to be a priest. What good would our love do for either of us?"

"Please let's enjoy the summer together. You'll have a new boyfriend as soon as school begins in the fall, so let me enjoy you for the summer. Is that okay with you?"

"Yes, it's okay with me. It's more than okay, I want to spend time with you too. This might be the last time in our lives we can be together."

THE LAST OF SYBIL NEWMAN??

The summer was flying by way too fast and I was spending more and more time with Syb. After the basement was finished, we had more time to ourselves. However, the time we all spent together completing the boy's apartment was one of the best times in my short life. Syb agreed it was loads of fun. She did say towards the end of the building project, she would like some alone time with me. I felt the same way.

We'd go to lake Hiawatha or lake Nokomis and would walk around those lakes hand in hand. We'd make out but had no sexual intercourse. We did some other things that Syb thought were appropriate for two young people in love. Whatever she was okay doing, I was more than okay.

Things at home were the best ever. Bud and Mom were really getting along. I was hoping they would tie the knot soon. It was quite evident that they loved one another by their hugging and kissing very indiscreetly. I loved watching them. They both had terrible lives before meeting each other. Bud had lost his wife early in life and well, Mom's life was just horrid.

I asked Mom point blank if she and Bud would be married soon. She replied, "Bud has asked me, and I just told him maybe. Mitchell, I just don't know if I want to try marriage again. The last one was so bad that it left me afraid to ever try it again. On the other hand, Bud is the nicest man I've ever met. I told him I needed more time to think about it. I'd like to just live like we are right now and maybe after you have finished your studies and you're ordained; I may consent to marriage."

"Mom, please get married now or in the near future. I have no idea about the priesthood right now. I don't want you to lose Bud. Please don't let him get away."

All Mom would say was, "I'll think about it."

As the end of summer was fast approaching Syb called me after work one Friday and asked me to come over. I quickly said, "Mom and Dad must be gone, I'll be right there."

She replied, "They're here. We'll sit in the backyard; I have a few things to tell you."

It sounded really serious, so I ran over immediately. I knocked on the front door and Mr. Newman just looked me over in disgust and said angrily "She's in the backyard waiting for you."

I walked around the corner of the house and Syb was sitting on a lawn chair crying her eyes out. She stuttered, "Mitch, please… come over…here and sit down…"

This didn't look good, but I sat right down. I said, "Are you okay? Did I do something to hurt you? What's wrong?"

Syb raised her voice and said, "Stop with all the damn questions. I can't see you any longer. I had a long talk with my folks, and they insist that we put an end this romance. They heard from Susie's mother Mrs. Benton, that we had sex when we were in grade school. My dad went off the deep end. That Susie Benton has been trying to get me in trouble for the last few years. Remember what she told Jimmy about me and you? Well, she told her mom the same stuff. And about me stealing the rubbers. I'm grounded for the rest of the summer and I cannot ever see you again. Our house will be on the market next spring and we're moving to Bloomington. I guess I don't really care about that, I'll be in college then."

I sat there in shock. What could I say, this is the worst thing that could happen to us? Her dad must want to kill me. I quietly said, "Did you deny the Benson accusations? What is wrong with that Susie? Oh Syb, I'm so sorry. I promise I'll stay away from you."

Syb dried her eyes in her hanky and said, "The worst part for me and my reputation. It's apparent that Susie and her mother have told everyone that would listen about us. Can you imagine what school will be like for me this fall. I'll be looked at as a whore and a slut. Mitch, what will I do?"

"Syb I just don't know. Does Susie think we are the only kids that tried sex? I bet she's had sex before. But I know that doesn't change things for you. I promise I'll stay away from you for the rest of your life. No calls, no letters, no nothing. Do you want to talk to your folks? I will, if you'd want me too."

"No! My God no! Things are bad enough around here. Please always remember, I love you so much. They can take you away from me physically but not mentally. I will always remember our times together and our love for one another."

As we both stood up and hugged, the back door swung open and I heard a voice scream loud and clear, "You get your damn hands off my daughter, you dirty Catholic! Some priest you'll make. I thought priests had to keep that damn thing in their pants, but not you. Get the hell away from my daughter and stay away. Maybe if you had an old man over there instead of all those losers hanging around, this travesty might not have happened. You and your family have always been the talk of the neighborhood and now you've added us to that status. Get out of my yard and stay away. If I see you in my yard or my house again, I'll shoot ya."

I stared at Mr. Newman but didn't utter a word. I turned very slowly and walked away. I could hear him yelling at Syb, "Get in the house this minute you little whore. Hugging that lowlife, not on my watch. What is wrong with you, get in the house?"

As Syb walked past her father she said loudly, "Did you forget Mom was pregnant with me when you got married. I guess the apple doesn't fall far from the tree. Did you call her a whore?"

I heard a loud slap and I turned to see Syb with her hand gently touching her right cheek. She had tears running down her face, but she said nothing. She walked slowly into the house. I didn't see her again.

The rest of the summer came and went. I did nothing but work and read. Kit and Mom wanted to know what happened to Sybil, but I just told them a few lies. Mom accepted all my lies about our breakup, but Kit didn't, she had heard the rumors. Kit finally found me in my room and walked in and closed the door. She said, "I think I heard what happened to you and Syb. Are the rumors true?"

"Yeah they're all true," I said. "Her mom and Dad went crazy about it and I must stay away from her permanently."

"Are you really going to do that?"

"Yeah, it's for the best. If I'm going to be a priest, why do it half-assed? I'm going to make an insidious endeavor to be a priest. I'm going to go all out in my endeavor."

Kit smiled, and replied, "Good for you, why would you want to do anything half-assed? I also have some news to share with you. Do you want to hear my news?" I just sat and shook my head yes. Kit continued, "Well, I'm not a virgin any longer. Mike and I had sex the other night near the point at lake Nokomis. It was wonderful and I can truly say I'm in love."

I stood up and hugged her and whispered in her ear, "I'm telling Mom."

Kit whispered back in my ear, "I already did."

"What? What, you told her? Why would you do such a thing? What did she say? I bet you got an earful."

"No, she was very nice about it. She said it was alright to do it with someone you love. And she hoped we would get married. She asked if we used protection and I said yes. She hugged me and said, 'I love Kit, you're a wonderful young lady.' Mitch, she's changed and she's very happy. I told her after you went back to school, she and Bud should share her bed. She thanked me and said they had planned on that already."

"Holy buckets! She said all that. Good for you Kit. And, you are a wonderful young lady and I'm so blessed to have you as my sister."

SENIOR YEAR

Summer ended and I had to return to Nazareth Hall for my senior year. We loaded Frank's old car with my clothes and other junk and Kit, Mom, Bud and I drove to the Hall. Once there, I checked into the dorm and there was little Davy Pearson standing by his bed. He said, "Welcome roommate. I hope you didn't mind that I asked to be your roommate?"

I replied, "Not at all. Davy, you grew. You must be twenty pounds heavier and how tall are you now?"

I'm five-foot-nine and I gained thirty pounds. I worked out all summer in hopes that our arch enemy Howie tries to bully me."

"You look great Davy. This is my mom, my sister Kit and my future dad Bud." After everyone was introduced my family left.

There was a slight knock on the door and Father O'Neil walked in. He said, "Good afternoon boys, how was your summer?"

Davy replied, "It was great Father, how was yours?"

"Uneventful. How about yours Mitchell?"

I pretended I didn't hear him, as I was unpacking. But he would not be detoured, he said again, "Mitchell, how was your summer?"

I never looked at him, I mumbled, "Okay."

He didn't say anything more, he just walked out of our room. Davy said, "Gees Mitch, that wasn't very nice. You've got to forgive and forget."

"No way Jose! Why should I forget that he wouldn't back me up? I've got nothing to say to him in the future. I can't wait until we graduate and get out of this dump."

"Mitch, have you heard they are considering closing Nazareth Hall in the next few years? Look around, there are hardly any kids left in this school. I hear their going to start a seminary school on the campus of Saint Thomas. We could be the last class that graduates from here."

I just replied, "Good!"

In the second week of school my mom called to tell me our friend Larry Hallstad had passed away. Larry had pancreatic cancer and had been sick for a long time. The funeral would be at OLPL on Saturday morning. Bud had moved into Mom's bedroom and Larry had the basement apartment all to himself. They found him one morning, he had died in his sleep. Larry had no real family left except us, so I knew I had to go home. Mom said she would have Kit pick me up around eight o'clock Saturday morning and wanted me to stay overnight.

I went to Father Rowen's office and asked to see him. The secretary said he was on his yearly retreat and wouldn't be back for a month. She said I needed to talk to Father Madison the assistant principal, who was temporally in charge in Rowen's absences. I peeked into Madison's office and he asked, "Yes, what do you want?"

I answered, "Father Madison, I've had a death in my family, and I must go home for the funeral this Saturday."

He reached into the file cabinet and asked, "Which family member, I see you have only two."

I replied, "Well, he wasn't a blood relative but a close family friend that lived with my sister and Mom. His name was Larry Hallstad."

"There in no one listed in your file by the name of Hallstad. So, you can't leave the dorm or the school for such nonsense."

"Nonsense? You think that a family friend's death is nonsense? Listen assistant principal, I'm going to that man's funeral no matter what you say. We were the only family he had left, so I'm going to be there for him."

"No, you're not! You can only leave the grounds of this school for a family emergency or a death in the family, he was not family. You can pray for him here where you belong at Nazareth Hall."

"You think you can keep me here? You forget, I can leave here anytime I want."

"You can drop out of our priesthood studies program permanently, but you'll not run off and see your little friends! Not on my watch."

I couldn't believe what I was hearing from this bloviating idiot. I was ready to attack him when I heard a quiet voice say, "Mitchell, have your family pick you up at the main entrance to our dorm. You have my permission to attend the funeral of your family friend. Please be back by eight o'clock Sunday night. I'm sorry for your loss." It was Father O'Neil. He was in his office next to Madison's office and had heard everything.

I took a huge breath and said, "Thank you father, this means a lot to me, he was a dear friend."

Madison screamed, "I'm in charge here, not you! This boy will not leave the grounds! I have strict rules to follow and he can only leave for family emergencies."

Father O'Neil again quietly replied, "Father Madison, Mitchell will be going home on Saturday morning with or without your permission. If you try and interfere, you'll have me to deal with. You likely don't know this but I spent most of my younger days living at the Boys Home Orphanage in south Minneapolis. It was a tough life that I endured at a young age. You also don't know the rest of my background. I was the middleweight golden gloves champ in the city of Minneapolis. I was a very good fighter, because I was a very angry young man. So, when I tell you something, which is not often, you'd best listen to me. If you don't, you will not like the consequences."

Madison responded by saying in an intimidating voice, "Are you threatening me?" O'Neil said nothing. But Madison screamed again, "Are you threatening me?"

Father O'Neil strode up to Madison and grabbed him by the throat and said, "Yeah, you little weasel, I'm threatening you. You'll not talk to me or any of the boys here at Nazareth Hall like this again. If you do, I'll beat you to an inch of your life. Don't underestimate me again, you don't understand my background or most of the backgrounds of the kids here. I will not tolerate bad behavior in a man, and this is bad behavior. Now step away from me and Mitchell."

I looked at Madison and he was really shaken up. O'Neil had scared the crap out of him. He backed up and said, "Alright, alright."

O'Neil said to me, "Mitchell, follow me." We walked to my dorm room both sat down. O'Neil then quietly said, "I'm sorry you had to hear all of that, but he is so out of line. I tried to back you up the last time, but Father Rowen would not allow it. This time I just couldn't stand by and see this so-called priest act this way. When Father Rowan gets back there will be a hearing and you'll be asked to testify. Be truthful and just tell it like it was. I'm going to be in trouble for this, but I just don't care."

I said, "Father, I'm so sorry I treated you poorly last year and in my room this year. I was mad at you for not standing up for me, but it sounds like you did. I'm really not sure about this priesthood thing any longer, especially after this run in with Madison."

"Please don't let this episode make you want to change your mind about becoming a priest. Wait until God sends you a message, then you'll know. Please for my sake, give it a chance."

As I waited for my ride, I promised myself I wouldn't utter a word about the problem I had of getting furloughed. Kit picked me up at eight o'clock sharp on Saturday morning. Mike Gorman had ridden along, and I was happy to see both of them. On the ride home I could see the love they had for one another. Kit giggled at everything Mike said, and I had to admit he was pretty funny.

I asked Kit about school and she said, "I didn't enroll at St. Cate's, I'm going to the University of Minnesota. They have a two-year nursing program and I'll be working in two years. After I get a paying job, I'll finish getting a four-year degree. Mike will be out of barber school in the next six months and he'll be working. So, we have news for you; we're getting married on December 2nd. It will be at OLPL and Father Bernard said he would come back and marry us."

I was stunned, I said, "Wow! This is a big surprise. What's the hurry?"

"Kit laughed and said, "I'm not pregnant if that's what you're insinuating. That will not happen until we have enough money to take care of a child."

"I was not insinuating anything like that, I was just surprised. And, I am very happy for both of you. I understand how much you love one another; I wish I could experience that. I'll be there."

Larry's funeral was short and sweet. There were just about ten other people that attended the service other than our family. We invited all of them to our house after the burial at Fort Snelling cemetery. Larry had been in the service; therefore, he could be buried at the veteran's cemetery. None of the others showed up at our house. It was quite a time for all of us, we knew we'd all miss Larry. I always figured it was Larry that brought all of us together.

I stayed overnight and Kit gave me a ride back to the Hall on Sunday morning. I told her, "This is going to be tough going back after spending such a nice day with you guys. Kit, I want you to know that I really like Mike a lot. I would, however, like to see you two wait a while before making such a big step. I realize the love you have for one another; I can see it in your faces and the way you treat each other. You're fun to watch. But school could be hard being married. Worrying about money will be a big obstacle in anyone's married life but at your ages it could end up being even more of an obstacle. I just want you to be happy and secure. If I had some money, I give it to you just so you wouldn't have to worry so much. I needed to get that off my chest, don't be mad."

Kit didn't immediately respond, but waited a few moments before saying, "Oh Mitch, you are so right. I'm going out of my mind with worry. I'm in love but having lived with Mom and Dad I realize there will be many problems. I'm scared out of my mind about this. When Mike proposed, I was so happy I immediately said yes, without thinking things through. After I've had time to think about it, it's just too soon. How do I tell him I want to wait? I know it will just kill him."

I said, "Kit, stop the car and turn it around. We're going back to Mike's house right now. I'll talk to him."

"What do you plan to say to him?"

"I'm going to tell him what you just told me. It's just too soon for you two to get married. You both need your education and Mike needs to build his business. If he loves you, he'll understand."

Kit stopped the car in front of Mike's house, and he ran out, he said, "What going on?"

I said, "Jump in the front Mike and Kit will you please get in the back, we've got to talk." After Mike got in, I went over everything Kit and I had talked about and all her questions about this marriage idea.

After I completed my diatribe, Mike turned and looked in the back seat where Kit was sitting and said, "You know Kit, Mitch is right. I didn't think this through. We need to wait until I get done with school and build a business. You need to get your education so we can save some money before having kids. The reason I wanted to get married right away is that I didn't want to lose you."

Kit smiled at Mike and just shook her head, "Lose me? Are you nuts? I'm so in love with you, you'll never lose me, but let's just wait."

Mike looked at me and said, "How did you get so smart? I think you'll make a great priest."

Kit and Mike drove me back to the Hall. I said my goodbyes and both of them hugged me and thanked me for helping them out. As I walked away, I thought, 'Neither of them wanted to get married now. After they agreed to get married, they thought there was no backing out. I'm glad I was there to help out.'

Now I had to face my own issues. Poor Father O'Neil could be drummed out of the priesthood for threatening another priest. I did like the way he handled that jerk Madison. It was quite evident that

Madison was scared, and he had a right to be. O'Neil had a tough life and he was a tough guy. You wouldn't know by looking at him, but he clearly showed his true colors. I wanted to talk to him, so I went to the rectory and asked at the front desk for him. Mrs. Arnold was the receptionist and was also working the switchboard when walked in. I waited for her to get off the phone before saying, "Hi, can I see Father O'Neil?"

She replied, "Are you Mitchell Collins? If so, I have a letter for you from Father O'Neil."

"Yes, I'm Mitchell Collins." I took the letter and I walked away.

When I got to my room, Davy was sitting on his bed reading a book, he looked up and said, "Boy you missed all the action around here. Father Madison and Father O'Neil got into a fight. O'Neil kicked the crap out of Madison."

I said loudly, "What! They had a fight?"

"Yeah, they did, right in the lunchroom. Madison walked in and screamed at O'Neil, 'You'll not threaten me ever again, if you do, I'll have you run out of the priesthood. If I have to, I'll go to Rome to have it done, I will.' O'Neil walked over to Madison and cold cocked. He dropped him to the floor and O'Neil stood over him and shouted, 'I see your mouth is the biggest thing on your body. Why don't you get up off the floor and we'll see how tough you are? Just remember I warned you.' Madison got up and took a roundhouse swing at O'Neil but missed by a mile. O'Neil hit him so hard his front teeth flew out of his mouth. Madison dropped to the floor crying like a baby."

"Holy crap! This was because of me. I've got to read this letter right away."

> Mitchell,
>
> Please forgive me for what I had done and please don't let this incident make you not want to be a priest. Father Madison and I got into a fight, well not exactly a fight, but I hit him a few times. He has been a thorn in my side for many years and I finally snapped. There is no excuse for

what I've done other than I just couldn't take it anymore. I'm leaving the priesthood immediately. I have pondered this move for several years now and the fisticuffs with Madison has made me believe it's time for me to move on. You are one of the shinning stars here at Nazareth Hall and I expect great things from you. I promise when I get settled, I'll contact you. You see I have a woman I left behind, and she needs me. Don't get the wrong idea, it's my mother. Hopefully, I will find someone that wants to love an old broken-down ex-priest. Drive hard Mitchell, you can be what ever you want in this life.

Ex-Father O'Neil

I read the letter over and over again. I now knew what Father was talking about, he wasn't sure he could stay in the priesthood. It now all made sense. He was fed up with the likes of Madison and likely Father Rowen too. He couldn't come out and tell me he had doubts about his continued role in the priesthood, but I think the way Madison and Rowen handled the Howie episode brought it to a head. I liked the way he ended the letter, telling me to drive myself hard and I could be whatever I wanted to be in life.

Father Rowen was called home from his retreat early, in order to quell the emotions that were running rampant after Father O'Neil resigned. I was called into the principal's office by Father Rowen. I walked in and sat down in the chair that Father had pointed at. He began, "What's all this I hear about you leaving the dorm last weekend for a non-family funeral? You know the rules, you are not allowed to leave unless it's an emergency."

"Well, I considered it an emergency as did Father O'Neil. A family friend that lived with us passed away and I was not going to miss his burial. If that's against the rules, the rules should be changed."

"Don't you ever talk to me in that condescending way again. I'm the principal here and you are nothing but a lowly student. Keep in mind that you are only here because I let you stay, after you beat that poor Howard to a pulp. So, if I were you, I'd shut that big mouth and listen to what I have to say. Bishop Manning will be here in the next couple of days and will want to interview you as to what happened with Father O'Neil. You'll do as I say and will not deviate to the script. Do you understand?"

"Yes Father."

"You will tell him about you fighting with Howard and how you've apologized to Howard and to the priests. You will also tell the bishop that Father O'Neil wouldn't listen to what I told him to be done about your punishment. You will also tell him how he threatened Father Madison. Do you understand?'

"Yes Father, I understand."

"Good, you may go back to your classes."

ALMOST OUT

I waited patiently for the bishop's visit to the Hall. It was not a couple of days out; it was a couple of weeks out. It appeared that Father O'Neil's departure was small potatoes to the esteemed bishop. When he finally showed up it was the week before Christmas. He spent many hours with Father Rowen and a much lesser amount of time with Father Madison, before they called witnesses. I was the first person to be called and I was prepared.

I walked into the principal's office and the bishop and Father Rowen were sitting together chatting and being cordial to one another. I was told by Rowen to sit down but was never formerly introduced to the bishop. Finally, the bishop said, "So, you are Mitchell Collins, is that correct?"

"Yes, I'm Mitchell Collins."

Rowen stood up and said, "You will address the bishop as the bishop or sir when you answer his questions."

I sat there with my hands on my lap looking at the bishop. He again addressed me, "So, I understand you were the instigator of an argument that took place with Father Madison and a former priest named Father O'Neil, is that correct?"

"Yes."

Rowen stood again and said, "What did I tell you? You'll address the bishop as bishop or sir when he asks you a question."

I finally had enough. I said, "Bishop, do you want me to answer some questions here or not? Could you please tell Father Rowen to leave the room so we can get this over with? He's very distracting and it's hard for me to concentrate with his constant interruptions and badgering."

"Lowell, will you please step outside? I'd like to talk to Mitchell alone." Rowen left in a huff. After he was out the door the bishop said, "How's that, he's gone? I want you to tell me the truth of what happened between O'Neil and Madison. The truth and only the truth. I want you to know I have an open mind about this, so just tell me what happened."

I began my testimony starting with last year and my fight with Howie. I then went on about Madison and Father O'Neil. I went into great detail and I ended with showing the bishop the letter Father O'Neil had left for me. After I completed my testimony, I just sat there waiting for the ax to fall. But it didn't.

The Bishop asked me a question, "Is your father Francis Collins and is your mother Bridget Collins, by any chance?"

"Yes, but my father passed away a couple of years ago."

"I met both of them when your father accused a priest of some misconduct. I won't go into details, but Father Bernard is an outstanding priest and he was falsely accused. Your mother verified that. But that's not what we're here for is it?"

"No Bishop, no sir, that's not what we're here for. I believe it's to cast Father O'Neil and I in a bad light. Isn't that the truth?"

The Bishop smiled and replied, "No it's not. Mitchell, as you can see, or at least I hope you can see, I'm very young to be a Catholic Bishop. I think I got the promotion because of my age. If you look around this archdiocese, there are mostly older men holding the higher positions within the church. They are set in their ways and they don't bend in the face of adversity. I'm hoping to change all of that. Your friend Father O'Neil is also a friend of mine. The reason I took so long coming here to Nazareth Hall was because of Patrick O'Neil. I needed to talk to him to find out why he left the priesthood. He told me the events exactly the way you described them. There are some things that are wrong here at Nazareth Hall and I intend to fix them."

I was stunned, to say the least. I finally had enough guts to responded, "Bishop Manning, Father O'Neil was a good priest and he didn't deserve the way he was treated. And that priest Madison, he's the worst. And, that Howie, this is no place for a kid like that. Now that's about all I have to say."

Bishop Manning laughingly said, "Mitchell my boy, you've indeed said enough. I promise I will make some changes here. And, I hope you will stay on and try to become a priest. Believe me when I say this, it's hard to complete this program. You have doubts and I had doubts. It's a normal thing because it's such a big step in your life. And, the priests and the teachers here at the Hall should be trained to understand what you boys are going through. Leaving your families at such a young age is a very difficult thing and not every boy is ready for it. I realize what you've gone through after meeting your father Francis. He was a difficult man. But you survived and over came all the roadblocks in your path. If you stay, you'll become a fine priest."

"What about Madison and Howie?"

"Father Madison has already been transferred out of the school and will no longer be a teacher. Some people are just not teacher material. Howard has been asked to leave the school. We have had so many complaints about that boy we could no longer allow him to be in this program. These changes should have happened long ago. We are also going to make some other changes here at the Hall. I would imagine that you boys all know we're in the process of closing the Hall permanently. But that's down the road a bit. Enrollment is way down and we can't afford to continue running it. Mitchell, it has been my pleasure meeting you and thank you for your candid response to my questions. You are a breath of fresh air here at the Nazareth Hall."

I stood up and shook hands with the bishop and thanked him. I then walked back to my dorm room.

I got back to my dorm room and Davy was waiting for me. He wanted to have a detailed explanation of what the bishop had to say. I sat down and went over everything he said, and Davy was mesmerized with what I had to say. He finally said, "Can you believe that someone around here finally believed you? That Madison was a jerk, I'm glad he's gone."

Our door opened and Howie walked in. He said, "Thanks to you Collins, I got kicked out of here. And you Davy, I'd like to kick your ass."

I stood up and walked towards Howie and said as he was backing up, "First off you stupid fool, you got yourself kicked out of here. You're not priest material. You and I both know that. You just wanted to get as far away from your mommy as you could. Living with her in a one-bedroom house must have been lots of fun. And home schooled by an idiot. Your educational background left all of us wondering if you ever went to school. We were right, you never went to a real school. You also bragged about all the women you shagged. We all realized that you didn't even know a girl in that godforsaken area you lived in. And for kicking Davy's ass, Davy and I'd like to see you try."

I had backed Howie up so far; he was standing half in our room and half in the hallway. He shook his head and said, "You guys don't know what you're talking about. My school had lots of kids. I was one of the toughest guys in my class too."

I laughingly said, "Yeah Howie, you are a real tough guy. I bet you and your mommy had lots of fights. I hope she wasn't the girl you had sex with."

Howie turned to walk away when Davy yelled, "Get back here Mr. Hard Guy, you said you wanted to lick my ass! Well here I am."

Howie continued to walk away as we laughed hysterically.

PREPARING FOR NEXT STEP

After things had quieted down a bit at the Hall, I was determined to go deeper into my religious studies. I knew my next step would be college and therefore I wanted to be prepared. I considered myself to be a good student, but with that in mind, the litmus test for me would be college. Could I survive the more rigorous curriculum that college demands?

Before I left Nazareth Hall, I wanted to study the Holy Ghost or now referred to as the Holy Spirit. It was always confusing to me that God was divided into three beings, the Father, Son and Holy Spirit. I could understand the Father and Son, but not the Holy Spirit. So, I went to my religious instructor Father Naslund's office, to have his help in explaining this phenomenon.

I explained to Father Naslund that I was confused and slightly dumbfounded about the role of this third person called the Holy Spirit. I asked when he or she was called the Holy Ghost and were they really referring to a ghost? If so, wouldn't that be kind of a frightening phenomenon?

Naslund explained, "First off, please call me Father Ron when we're in my office. Now, I'll try and give my explanation of the Holy Spirit and where the term came from; the Hebrew Bible first refers to the 'Spirit of God.' That term also is the equivalent to the expression of 'Spirit of the Lord,' found in rabbinical literature. In the Old Testament, Genesis 1:2, states, 'God's spirit hovered over the form of lifeless matter, thereby making creation possible.' It would seem that the Jews believed the Holy Spirit was a kind of communication medium like the wind."

Father Ron then picked up his bible and looked over his notes within its pages and said, "In the New Testament the term Holy Spirit appears around ninety times. The sacredness of the Holy Spirit to Christians is affirmed in three of gospels of Matthew, Mark and Luke. Those gospels proclaim that blasphemy against the Holy Spirit is an unforgivable sin. Jesus himself says in the Gospel of Matthew, "Go ye therefore, and make disciples of all nations, baptizing them into the name of the Father and the Son and the Holy Spirit."

Father Ron continued, "The Holy Spirit does not just appear for the first time after the resurrection of Jesus, but it's mentioned in a gospel of Luke, prior to Jesus being born. In Luke 1:15, John the Baptist was said to be 'filled with the Holy Spirit,' prior to the birth of Jesus, and the Holy Spirit came upon the Virgin Mary in Luke 1:35. In Luke 3:16 John the Baptist stated that Jesus was baptized not with water but with the Holy Spirit; and the Holy Spirit descended upon Jesus during his baptism. Luke 11:13 also says Jesus provided assurances that God the Father would give the Holy Spirit to those who ask him."

This was my own private lecture on the Holy Spirit. It was now that I understood where the term Holy Spirit came from but, I was still a bit confused. I also understood that I had to believe this part of the bible if I were to continue into the next phase of the priesthood.

Father Ron said, "Mitch, in Mark 13:11, he refers to the power of the Holy Spirit to act and speak through the disciples of Jesus in time of need: 'be not anxious beforehand what ye shall speak: but whatsoever shall be given you in that hour, that speak for ye; for it is not ye that speak, but the Holy Spirit.' This means that when the disciples were preaching the word of God, the Holy Spirit would be speaking through the disciples himself. Luke's Acts of the Apostles contain over half of the references in the New Testament to the Holy Spirit and Luke wrote approximately 25% of the contents of the New Testament. The Acts of the Apostles has sometimes been referred to as 'Book of the Holy Spirit' or 'Acts of the Holy Spirit.' One last thing, the New Testament details a close relationship between the Holy Spirit and Jesus during the early days of His ministry. The Gospels of both Matthew and Luke state Jesus was 'conceived by the Holy Spirit, born of the Virgin Mary.' Mitch, I could go on and on about the Holy Spirit, but the one thing, you as a Catholic you must believe is, God the Father, Jesus the Son and the Holy Spirit. The Holy Spirit is the third person in the Trinity."

I was shaken and very confused, I replied, "Father Ronald, you've given me a lot to think about. Clearly the bible refers to the Holy Spirit over and over again, much more than I realized. I'll continue my reading, but I will concentrate more than before."

"Mitch, it's all right to have doubts, all of us have doubts. But remember what Jesus said in Bible according to John, 'Because you have seen me, you have believed. Blessed are those who have not seen and yet believe.'"

Again, I was surprised. Father Ron knew the bible and knew it very well. If I were to become a priest, I would also have to be an expert on the bible. I thought, 'Man, I'd better get moving and read all this stuff again and get help interpreting all of it.' I said, "Thanks for all your help Father Ron, I promise I'll be back, I still have lots of questions."

GRADUATING

School was as good as expected. It was really nice having Davy as my roommate. He had a dry sense of humor and was really smart. He was beginning to have doubts about becoming a priest, however. We talked often about the bible and about the Catholic Church. He used to say, "There is so much I just don't believe in. And Mitch, I think I want to find a woman and fall in love and have some babies like my folks did."

I told Davy about my conversation with Father Ron and said he should go and see him, as I did.

Davy's response was, "I don't need a lesson on the bible or a lesson on interpretation of the said bible. I understand all of that. It's that my heart isn't into all of this any longer. Can't you understand that? Even you have doubts. I'm going to finish the rest of my year here, but I will take the summer off to contemplate my future."

I said in return, "You know that's a good idea for both of us. I think I'll go home again and work at the school and figure out what I want out of life. I also want to see if my old friend Leanna is still around. I had so much fun with her my last year at OLPL."

Davy replied, "What about the fair Sybil? Is she completely out of the picture?"

"I'm afraid she is. Her parents found out about our sexual experiences with one another and they are moving out of the neighborhood. At least they were going to move by next summer. You know Davy, I still love her and if she loved me and we were older, I'd be out of here in a heartbeat."

"I think you should reevaluate your position on the priesthood. If you love someone as you do, what are the chances of you being a priest long term?"

"Davy, she'll never think of me once she's out of high school. She a beautiful woman and she'll have her pick of all the good looking, athletic guys in college. She won't ever think of me again."

Our Nazareth Hall class had sixteen boys graduate this year. Only about half would attempt to continue to the seminary. It was no wonder the school was closing. Graduation day was fun. Mom, Bud, Kit and Mike attended the graduation. After the mass and the ceremony was completed, we were walking towards Bud's car, when a familiar voice said, "Hey Mitch, congratulations, it's nice to see you again."

It was Father O'Neil, oops, Patrick O'Neil and he was standing there with a very pretty young woman. I said, "Mr. O'Neil, did you come all the way here just to see me graduate?"

"Call me Pat, or Patrick, not Mr. anything. Mitch, this young, beautiful woman, is my wife of one week, Judy O'Neil."

I smiled and said, "Judy, it's so nice to meet you. I figured Patrick had a lady in waiting after he left. It's so nice to meet you. This is my family, my mom Bridget, her main squeeze Bud, my sister Kit and her main squeeze Mike."

Judy smiled at all of us very coyly before saying, "Patrick and I didn't know each other until very recently. I did not know him before, or during his stay in the priesthood."

I realized I had made a huge faux pas. I began to sweat a bit and embarrassingly said, "Judy, I'm so sorry for what I said. I didn't mean that really, I didn't. I was not suggesting you two were seeing each other while Patrick was a priest. Please forgive me."

Pat hugged Judy close to his body and said, "Mitch, please don't apologize it's not your fault. We have had so many do-gooders insinuate that we knew each other all along, but we didn't. We met at a bible study class at Saint Bartholomew. Judy had been divorced and wanted clarity on what the bible says about divorce."

Judy quietly said, "Can we all go somewhere and talk about this. It's very embarrassing for me to talk about this in public."

I said, "Mom, I'll ride with Pat and Judy and we'll follow you to our house. Is that okay with you guys?"

Mom shook her head yes. I then got into the backseat of Pat's car. I said, "Judy, I wish I could take back what I said. I guess I said that because of a girl that I loved, and I'd leave the priesthood in a heartbeat if she came back into my life."

Judy was smiling when she said, "That was nice to hear. I am divorced and I also had my marriage annulled. Having it annulled; means I was never married in the eyes of the church. But it never felt like I was really ever married the way it was. The guy I married didn't want to be married any longer. It got to the point where we didn't like each other anymore. When I met Pat, it was love at first sight. He was out of the priesthood for only six months when we met. We were married three months later."

Pat said, "This has been the best part of my life so far. Believe me when I say this: I did love the priesthood, but I hated the bureaucracy of it. Mitch, you saw the bureaucracy firsthand with Madison and Rowen. They've been priests for so long they lost touch of people's feelings and they would not bend their mandated insipid rules. They pushed me out of the priesthood and I gladly left. I just couldn't take any more of them."

"I met Bishop Manning recently and he told me that he knew you very well. And, he also said he got Madison out of the Hall and he can't teach again. Howie was also kicked out but I'm not sure about Rowen."

Patrick and Judy both laughed at my comments. Patrick said, "Jim Manning and I were in the seminary together and we're very close friends. In fact, he married Judy and I."

I was stunned, I stuttered, "He married… you… two? I'm shocked! I didn't know bishops married anyone. You called him Jim?"

"That's his name Mitch. You mentioned Father Rowen, he's out as of today. Jim took care of that too but gave him until the end of the school year to resign. Jim called it saving face."

We pulled up in front of our house and Patrick said, "Are you sure you want us to go in?"

I laughed and said, "You bet I do. You have been the best thing in my life for a very long time. I want to celebrate with you and Judy. And Judy, you are a lucky woman to get a good man like Patrick."

I was planning on working at OLPL this summer to get enough money for college or the seminary. I was also hoping on seeing the lovely Syb this summer. My dreams of seeing her diminished immediately, when sister Kit informed me that her parents had sold their house and had moved to Bloomington. Kit spoke to her on her moving day. She told Kit that she was going to attend Mankato State college in the fall. She planned now to become a teacher.

I called my friend Leanne and asked her if we could get together for a movie or just to make out. She laughed before saying, "Not on your life Mitch. I'm going steady with a guy named Harry Daly and the last thing I want is to lose him over a priest. You do realize that priests cannot make out with a woman, don't you? Mitch, I really liked you, but we have no future together. Have a nice summer and good luck in the seminary."

THE SEMINARY

After being shot down by Leanne, I felt all alone again. It seemed like that's the way I've felt most of my life. So, I did the first thing that came into my mind, I began to prepare for the seminary. I was now determined to become a priest. The only two girls in my life that mattered had moved on, so would I. I made up my mind that I would get my undergraduate degree in three years or less. That degree would be in philosophy. In graduate school I would work on a master's in theology with a focus on Biblical research. That degree is commonly called a Master of Divinity.

I worked the summer at OLPL, and I had absolutely no social life. Bud and Mom had gotten hitched and were very happy. I worked alongside of Bud all summer and we got along very well. I'd see Leanne several times this summer and she would only wave and walk away.

In the fall, I began my college career at Saint John Vianney College Seminary (SJV), on the upper campus of St. Thomas College in St. Paul Minnesota. The classes were structured around the Bible, theology, philosophy and other required studies such as, English, Latin, history, mathematics, etc.

I dove headfirst into my studies and I blocked all social events out of my mind. All I did was study. I was bound and determined to be the top student in the seminary, and I was. My goal to graduate in three years was going to happen come hell or high water.

I was told continuously by the staff of priests to slow down and digest everything they were teaching me. I just couldn't slow down. I thought I was grasping everything they taught me, but I clearly was not. I'd ace every test, but I rarely understood the material. The Bible was my nemesis. I just couldn't understand the Old Testament. I felt it was written by some old farts two thousand years ago and nothing in it pertained to life today. There are 613 commandments that the Jews followed in the Old Testament. Some of the commandments pertained to not eating pork. Big deal.

Then there is the Seven Laws of Noah; 1. Do not worship idols, 2. Marry to have children, 3. Do not commit adultery, 4. Do not consume blood, 5. Do not steal, 6. Do not murder, 7. Do not bear false witness. In summary; The Seven Laws include prohibitions against worshiping idols, cursing God, murder, adultery and sexual immorality, theft, eating flesh torn from a living animal, and the obligation to establish courts of justice.

Then the rules of Leviticus list the dietary restrictions God gave to the nation of Israel, they are, prohibition against eating pork, shrimp, shellfish and many types of seafood, most insects, scavenger birds and many other animals.

But verse in the Old Testament again by Leviticus 20:13, was the one on homosexuality had me confused. 'If there is a man who lies with a male as those who lie with a woman, both of them have committed a detestable act. God's Word says the homosexual act is detestable; it is an abomination.'

Wow! I have to say that I know for a fact, that there are several homosexual men here in the seminary. They are good men and they cause no trouble and I don't see them as an abomination. I wonder how they feel when they read the Old Testament. I also wonder, if this is so wrong, why did God make them like that? They didn't have a choice to be a homosexual did they, God just made them that way? I'm confused about all of this, so I've given up on trying to understand the Old Testament.

I realized quickly when reading the New Testament that there are very few references to homosexuality. The only reference is by Paul in his letter to the Romans and there is speculation that he himself was a homosexual. Not that I care and there is no actual proof.

One of the things that had drawn me to the New Testament was the Sermon on the Mount. It was a time when the crowds were beginning to follow Jesus early in His Ministry. It takes place after Jesus had been baptized by John the Baptist and he had finished fasting and meditating in the Judaean Desert. The Sermon is Jesus longest dissertation found in the New Testament. The things I liked about this part of the New Testament, is that Jesus focuses on love and humility, rather than force and damnation. It speaks volumes of his highest ideals in his teachings on spirituality and compassion.

The beatitudes are his teachings of love and compassion, some of them are as follows;

1. Blessed are the poor in spirit, for theirs is the kingdom of heaven.
2. Blessed are those who mourn for they will be comforted.
3. Blessed are the meek, for they will inherit the earth.
4. Blessed are those who hunger and thirst for righteousness, for they will be filled.
5. Blessed are the merciful, for they will be shown mercy.
6. Blessed are the pure of heart, for they will see God.
7. Blessed are the peacemakers, for they will be called children of God.
8. Blessed are those who are persecuted because of righteousness, for theirs is the kingdom of heaven.
9. Blessed are you when people insult you, persecute you and falsely say all kinds of evil against you because of me. Rejoice and be glad, because great is your reward in heaven, for in the same way they persecuted the prophets who were before you.

Jesus, in my opinion, made some profound statements here. This has become the crux of my beliefs as a Catholic, love and compassion.

Jesus also taught us how to pray while giving the Sermon on The Mount. He said, 'And when you pray, do not be like the hypocrites, for they love to pray standing in the synagogues and on the street corners to be seen by others. Truly I tell you, they have received their reward in full. But when you pray, go into your room close the door and pray to the Father, who is unseen. Then your Father, who sees what you have done in secret, will reward you. And when you pray, do not keep on babbling like pagans, for they think they will be heard because of their many words. Do not be like them, for your father knows what you need before you ask him. This then, is how you should pray:'

'Our Father in Heaven,
hallowed be your name,
your kingdom come,
your will be done'
on earth as it is in heaven.
Give us today our daily bread.
And forgive us our debts,
as we also have forgiven our debtors.
And lead us not into temptation,
but deliver us from the evil one.'

'For if you forgive other people when they sin against you, your heavenly Father will also forgive you. But if you do not forgive others their sins, your Father will not forgive your sins.'

So, in my studies so far, I have come away with a fondness for the New Testament, but I do not see much sense in the Old Testament

GRADUATION

My undergraduate degree was completed in two and half years. I was first in the class ahead of me that graduated in four years' time. I had immersed myself in my studies and I had no social life at all. I became an academic hermit. Kit and Mike would visit me once a month and they were always so lovely dovey all the time. It made me sick. Just kidding, I was jealous, to say the least. I would always ask Kit if she had seen Sybil. And she always replied she had not. I also asked her about Leanne. She had seen her, and she was in love with a very nice guy named Harry. Kit thought that he was either a Negro or Italian, she couldn't figure out which.

On my graduation day no one came to the event. I just didn't tell my family I was graduating, they all thought I had a year and half left. I attended the mass and received my diploma, which stated I was number one in the class and a merit scholar. Big deal! I didn't even have a friend to share my accomplishments with, nor family.

I had just turned twenty-one, so I could drink legally now. So, after the ceremony I went straight to a bar called, Standup Steve's. It was rightly called Standup Steve's, because there were no chairs, bar stools or tables, you just stood at one of the three bars. I had never really drank any hard liquor before, but I thought this would be a good time to drown my sorrows. I ordered a rum and coke, but much to my chagrin, the bartender said, "We don't serve pussy drinks in here. Ya want some whiskey?"

I was embarrassed to say the least, so I said, "Can I have a whiskey and coke?"

The barkeep responded, "Whiskey and water it is then."

The barkeep set the drink in front of me and it was so dark I thought he gave me a glass of coffee. I took a sip and almost choked. I took steady small sips and when it was all gone the barkeep said, "You want me to keep um coming?"

I was feeling pretty good about then, so I said, "You bet your ass, keep um coming."

I was on my third whiskey water when a good-looking older lady stood by me and asked, "Hi their sweetie, would you buy a lady a drink?"

I slurred out the words, "Youuuu betcha. Whatcha drinking?"

"How about a shot of Jack and a Grain Belt chaser."

I said to the barkeep, "My friend will have a hack and a drain belt."

The woman said to the barkeep, "Billy, Jack and a grain chaser."

I said, "Yeah, Jack and grain. Whatcha name baby?"

"Debbie, what's yours, big guy?"

"Call me Mitch."

"What do you do Mitch, for a living?"

"Well, I going to be a priest. That's what I do."

"Yeah, and I'm going to be a nun."

The barkeep laughed and said, "Can nuns be hookers?"

I looked at the barkeep and I could hardly see him through all the smoke in the bar. I said, "What's a hooker?"

He replied, "She is, young Debbie here. When I say young, she's a young forty."

Debbie gulped down her shot of Jack and said laughingly, "Bull crap, I'm only twenty-two and ain't never been missed."

I was really confused; I didn't get their jokes and I was getting sick to my stomach. I turned to go to the men's room, and I puked all over Debbie and the floor. The next thing I knew, I was thrown out of the bar, but before that, they took all the money out of my wallet and slapped me silly. I sat on the street with puke running down my shirt and mouth. I got up slowly to walk back to campus when a squad car stopped me from going across the busy street. The cop that was driving said, "Get in the backseat kid, you're too drunk to walk home alone in this neighborhood."

I wondered where the cop was going to take me, so I slobbered, "Are you taking me to jail?"

The cop was a nice man, he said, "We're going to take you home. Where is home?"

I said, "I hate to say this, but I'm in the seminary at St. Thomas."

The cop replied, "Yeah, you're gonna be a priest. Now, where do you live?"

I sat in the backseat and began to cry. I don't know why I was crying, but I just couldn't stop. I think everything in my life had just come to a head. I was alone, so all alone. I told the cop, "Can you take me to my mom's house, it's in south Minneapolis."

The cop replied, "I get off in a half hour. After I tie up at the station, I'll give you a ride home. By the way, what is your name?"

"My name is Mitch Collins, what's yours?"

"Call me Ted. Ted Boran. I live in Minneapolis so it's not out of my way. Mitch, what the hell is a squared away kid like you doing in a shithole bar like Standup Steve's?"

"I don't know. I just graduated from college and I went out to celebrate; Standup Steve's was the closest bar around. As you can tell I'm not a very good drunk."

Ted drove me to the police station, and he went in to do his paperwork. I waited in the parking lot by his car. He drove me home and when I got there, I had sobered up a bit. Ted asked me, "Are you gonna be okay?"

I replied, "Yeah, I think so. My mom will be upset with me, but I just don't care anymore."

Ted grabbed a piece of paper from a tablet and wrote his phone number on it. He said, "Listen, if you need some help in the future call me. And, if you need someone to talk to call me. Okay?"

I thought, 'Wow, a cop with a personality and one that is willing to help someone after work, without getting paid. "Thanks Ted, for your help. I don't know what I'd have done without your help."

I opened the car door and got out as Ted drove away. The front door to mom's house opened and Kit walked out and I could tell she was confused. She walked slowly to where I was standing and said, "Mitch, what are you doing here? And, what happened to you? You're a mess. Have you been sick?"

I smiled at her and said, "Hi Kit. Yeah, I've been sick. Sick of life." I began to cry again. I cried so hard I stumbled and then fell to the ground. I sat on the ground crying my eyes out. Kit dropped to the ground and embraced me in her arms and held on tightly to me. I couldn't stop crying. I then realized Kit was crying too. Here we were in front of our house, both crying our eyes out and neither of us knew why.

After about ten minutes of bawling, we looked at each other and began to laugh. Now we were laughing so hard we couldn't stop. My dear God, how I missed my big sister. She was the only one in the world that understands me. After a while we got up and walked into an empty house. Kit got me a clean shirt from Bud's closet, and we sat down to discuss life.

Kit wiped her tears away and finally said, "What's wrong? I hate when you're so upset, it tears me apart."

I smiled at her; it was nice knowing someone really cared about me. I replied, "Kit, I graduated from college today and I was all by myself. It took me only two and half years and no one cared. Not one person has ever asked me about college or how I was doing. And, whether I was happy or if I was having fun. Well, I'm not happy and I'm not having fun. All I've done in the last couple of years was study. I hate my life and you are the only person that cares about me. Our mother, CB only now cares about Bud and herself. She forced me into the priesthood and then ignored me. I haven't seen her in over nine months."

"Oh, my goodness Mitch. You're not serious? She hasn't been there in nine months? I'm so sorry. I should have come more often too, but with school and Mike, I just couldn't get there. I promise I'll come every week from now on."

"Kit, it's not good for you to come every week, you have a life, I don't. This is the life I chose, and I have to live with that decision. Can you give me a ride back to prison?"

Kit said, "Mom and Bud are gone for the day and Mike is working. Can you stay here for the night and Mike and I will give you a ride tomorrow? I want to spend some time with you today even though you're still pretty drunk."

"I'll stay, I want to talk to you too and I'm not drunk any longer. I think I puked all the booze out of me at the bar. Can I sleep downstairs in one of the new bedrooms?"

"I think that will be alright, however, keep in mind that is my domain now. I took over the downstairs apartment a year ago. Mike and I have gotten to know each other very well down there, if you get my meaning?"

"I get it, but it's a little more information than I need to know. Aren't you worried about getting pregnant?"

Kit laughed and said, "Where have you been, living under a rock? Haven't you heard about birth control pills? It's all the rage for us young single girls. It prevents having a baby until you want one. And, I don't want one yet. Also, the Catholic church condemns all kinds of birth control other than the rhythm method, which doesn't work."

"You say the church is against birth control pills? Why? I would submit to you, that preventing an unwanted pregnancy is much better than bringing an unwanted child into this world. I wonder, does the church believe that people should just not have sex? God made them to want and to have sex. I've come to realize the church needs to do some serious thinking about all these things. When I become pope, I'll address all of these issues."

Kit smiled and said, "Yeah, you being the pope. Did you forget you've already had sex? The pope could never, ever have had sex. You disqualified yourself before the College of Cardinals has had a chance to vote on you." Kit and I sat and talked for hours. We heard Mom and Bud come home but we never told them I was there.

The next morning Mike picked Kit and I up at six o'clock in the morning, long before Mom and Bud woke up. I told Kit to say hello for me.

GRADUATE SCHOOL

Kit and Mike had left me off at my dorm early that next morning. Later in the day, I got a call from my mother Bridget. She wanted to know why I didn't tell her and Bud about my graduation ceremony. She also wanted to know why I didn't tell them that it took me only two and half years to complete my degree. I laughed at her and said, "Mother, you never asked me about school, never, ever. You never encouraged me or asked me any questions about my life since you met Bud. I'm okay with that, but please don't call me now and act like you're concerned. You had your chance. Please just leave me alone, I'm an academic hermit now and I don't need you or anyone else in my life. You spent most of my life telling me I would be a priest, whether I wanted to or not, so you've gotten your wish. Now you and Bud go and live your lives the way you want, and I will live my life, also the way you wanted me to. Goodbye Bridget, please don't call me again."

As I hung up, I heard her sobbing. I just couldn't take this BS anymore. She got what she wanted and it's too late for me to change now. I told Kit what I was going to say to Bridget, and she was okay with it. I was okay as long as Kit was still in my life. I now realized that Kit was more than a sister, she was like the mother I never had. I would never tell her that, she'd remind me that she is only two years older than me.

The next phase in my education was my master's degree. I was certain I could complete it in approximately three to three and half years. The classwork would include more philosophy classes, several years of graduate level seminary formation in theology, with a focus on Biblical research. Hopefully I would end with a Master of Divinity. Again, I immersed myself in my studies. I worked harder than anyone in the seminary and I had no social life, unlike the other potential priest. My professors were concerned that I was becoming a recluse and that was not a good trait for a priest. A priest, besides being scholarly, must have great communication skills. I thought I possessed both needed skills, but Kit assured me that I needed to get out and meet people and have some fun. I clearly remembered when the last time I fun had; it was with Sybil or with Leanne. Women, the forbidden fruit for priests.

I was intrigued with the philosopher Saint Thomas Aquinas. He was a theologian and a scholastic philosopher. He considered all philosophers, however, as pagans because they all fell short of what he thought was the true and proper wisdom to be found in Christian revelations. Thomas Aquinas believed, 'That for the knowledge of any truth whatsoever man needs divine help, that the intellect may be moved by God to its act.' He believed that man had the capacity to know things without any divine revelation, even though such revelations do not occur very often, but they do occur in regard to truths pertaining to faith. In other words, through God we can understand most things related to our faith.

According to Thomas, all acts of virtue are prescribed by natural law. Since each one's reason naturally dictates to him to act virtuously. He defined four cardinal virtues as prudence, temperance, justice and fortitude. There are three theological virtues too, they are faith, hope and charity. The perfect virtue is charity. He says, 'non-Christians can display courage, but it would be courage with temperance. A Christian would display courage with charity.' My thoughts on this are the same as my thoughts on the Old Testament, I just don't believe all of it. Thomas is saying that if you are not a Christian, you cannot be a charitable person. It's always the same, they always disparage other faiths and other views.

When I was younger, the priests and the nuns in our parish, told us that other religions were false religions and the only true religion was the Catholic religion. I could never understand why there were so many Protestant, Lutheran, Jewish and Episcopalian churches and synagogues around my house. What was wrong with all those people? They were at the wrong church; didn't the Catholics tell them that? I just didn't get it and I still don't. I respect every one's religion as long as they believe in something. The American Indians believed in a Spirit that resided in animals or in nature. Is that wrong? I think not. At least they believed in a superior being. I am reminded all the time that I am going to be a Catholic priest, therefore, I must believe all that the Church tells me to believe. I'm having a difficult time with all of this.

I continued my education in a feverish pace, and I increased my workload until the professor's would not allow me to do anymore. They felt I was overdoing things trying to complete my education in too much of a hurry. I slowed down quite a bit but was still on my way to completing my education in three years or less.

I was instructed on the duties of a priest and some of them are as follows; a priest is required to recite the Liturgy of the Hours daily, also known as the Divine Office or the Work of God. This is the daily prayer of the Church, marking the hours of each day and sanctifying the day with prayer. The Hours are a meditative dialogue on the mystery of Christ, using scripture and prayer.

A priest who becomes a pastor is responsible for the administration of a Catholic parish. The Church, his living quarters and possibly a school would all be on the premises. The priest's duty is to provide to the spiritual needs of the Catholics that belong to that parish. This would include performing ceremonies for the seven sacraments of the church and counseling parishioners.

The seven sacraments are efficacious signs of grace, instituted by Christ Himself and entrusted to the Church. The seven sacraments are; Baptism, Eucharist, Confirmation, Confession or Reconciliation, Administering the Last Rights, Marriage and Holy Orders.

I realized the Church wants its priests to be intelligent and well educated, but also have human, social, spiritual and pastoral qualities. The instructors tell us that the purpose of our seminary education is to ultimately prepare students to be pastors of souls. I felt I was ready.

I attended classes throughout the entire school year and I also attended classes all summer. I was working on obtaining my degree before my twenty-fifth birthday. In 1975, at age twenty-five, I had completed my education and was ready to be ordained into the priesthood.

The Rite of Ordination is what makes a priest a priest. The Ordination occurs within the context of the Holy Mass. After we were called forward and presented to the congregation, we were all interrogated. We all promised to perform the duties of the Priesthood and to respect and obey the bishop or our religious superior. We finally lay prostrate before the alter, while the assembled congregation knelt and prayed for the help of all the saints in singing the Litany of the Saints.

The most important part of the rite is when the bishop silently laid his hands on each of us candidates, before offering the consecratory prayer, addressed to God the Father, invoking the power of the Holy Spirit upon those of us being ordained. After the consecratory prayer, we newly ordained priests were given vestments, which included a chasuble and stole. Then the bishop anointed our hands with chrism before presenting us with our own chalice and paten, which we will use when presiding at the Holy Eucharist. Chrism is a mixture of oil and balsam, which I'll use for baptisms and other anointing. The chalice and paten were given to me by my mother and Bud and both were very ornate. The chalice is made of gold and will hold the Holy Eucharist, and the paten is a plate also made of gold, that will cover the chalice and will be used as protection against dropping the Holy Eucharist while serving communion.

After my ordination into the priesthood, Mom, Bud, Mike, Kit and I went out for dinner. Mom was all smiles, but Kit was not. She hardly spoke and hardly ate anything. Mom and Bud had to leave early and that left Mike, Kit and I at the table. I asked, "Now, what is wrong with you my big sister? Is it something I said?"

Kit had tears in her eyes, and said, "This is so wrong. So wrong. This is the last thing you ever wanted to be, was a priest. I let you down. I should have insisted that you go to Roosevelt high school for three years before deciding to go into the seminary. What thirteen-year-old kid is ready to make this big of a decision for a lifetime job? I tried it myself and I just couldn't do it. It's just not right."

"Kit, I'm sorry you're blaming yourself for my decision, and it was my decision. Yes, what kid knows what he or she wants to be at thirteen? I still don't. I will tell you both this, I will try my hardest to make this work. I'm educated and I know the priestly rules and I'll try and follow them. As you know I have my doubts, but I hope I can perform my duties while still having those doubts."

Kit smiled at me as she wiped away her tears. She replied, "Mitch, you'll be a great priest, where will you be stationed?"

"I'll find out tomorrow where I'll be stationed. I hope it's a small church, but I fear it will be one of the larger parishes, one where they'll have several assistant pastors. Wherever it is, I hope I'll be able to see you two guys once in a while. It will have to be in the Twin Cities, at least I hope it is."

I hugged my sister Kit and shook hands with her future husband Mike. I was off to begin a new life. I felt I was prepared to be a priest, but I soon found out I was not prepared at all for the life of what I refer to as a hermit priest. Meaning no wife, no kids and no family.

FIRST ASSIGNMENT

I got my assignment early Monday morning and I wasn't surprised. Saint Clément's in south Minneapolis is a very large church, with over one thousand families in the congregation. I had never heard of the Saint Clement of Rome and I thought it would be best if I found out about him. So, I went to the library and looked him up. I found very little about his life except that he was supposed to have been the pope in the late 1st century. It was to have been said, that he was concentrated by Peter himself and he was the second or third pope. The story also stated that Clement was imprisoned under Emperor Trajan of Greece; during that time, he was reported to have led a ministry of fellow prisoners. He was executed by being tied to an anchor and thrown into the sea. He became the patron saint of mariners. Why he would have had his named attached to a church in Minnesota is a mystery to me. It's an old church, so maybe the founders were from sea bearing areas of the world. I guess I don't know, and I could care less.

I reported for duty on a Monday morning and asked the housekeeper if I could see Pastor Wiggins. I followed her to a main floor office, and she rapped on the door. I heard a voice say, "I'm not to be disturbed, I'm saying my morning prayers."

The housekeeper replied, "But Father, your new assistant pastor is here waiting to meet you."

Pastor Wiggins in his most religiously voice yelled back, "What did I say woman? I'm not to be disturbed I'm saying my lauds. That means morning prayers. So, get away from the damn door before I fire you. And tell that young man out there with you, he should take this time to also recite his lauds too. Now, leave me alone!"

I was stunned. I'd never in all my years in the seminary heard a priest talk like that. This man is the pastor of a very large church and he's yelling at this poor woman. I could tell she was worried about losing her job, so I said, "I'm so sorry about this. I'll leave and I'll come back later. Is he like this all the time?"

She shook her head yes and I could see a tear running down her cheek. She replied, "Yes, he is so mean. I do this job for nothing, it's my charitable contribution to the Church. But I'm getting to the end of my rope. I'm thinking about finding another way to contribute to the Church. This is clearly not working."

"How long have you worked here?"

"Six years, a very long six years."

"If I were you, I'd quit. And before I did, I tell him what a jerk he is."

I looked at her and she was laughing. She was laughing very hard. She said, "I like you Father Mitch. I want to stay around and see how you handle this old fart."

"What is your name?"

"Agnes Winter is my name. My husband Al, God rest his soul, died ten years ago. I do this job in remembrance of him. Al was a strong Catholic, much stronger than I."

"You called me Father Mitch. I like that. I think that's what I'll call myself, Father Mitch. Thanks Agnes, I think you and I will be good friends."

Agnes replied, "Well Father Mitch, let me show you to your room, it's upstairs."

We walked up a flight of stairs and my room was the first one on the right. It was the smallest room I'd ever seen. There was a very small bed, a nightstand with a small lamp on it, a small dresser and the smallest closet I'd ever seen. It had no windows, no curtains, no nothing. I started thinking, this room is very apropos for me the hermit priest. I laughed to myself as Agnes left me alone to my closet bedroom. I thought, 'I bet Father Wiggins has stately quarters, very big and fit for a king. Screw him, I'll take the room and just shut up about it. I'm sure his reason for giving me this room was to show me that he was the boss. I admit he's going to be the boss. I hate him already and I hadn't even met him face to face. Hate is too strong of word, I disliked him personally, that's all. I'm sure God would forgive me for disliking someone.'

Two hours later as I was sitting on a bench in the yard, the door to the rectory opened and the esteemed Father Wiggins yelled, "Get in here! Get in here now!"

I walked slowly to the rectory and walked into a fuming Pastor Wiggins. He yelled again, "When I tell you to do something you do it. When you're told to get in here, I expect you to run. Do you understand?"

I responded, "You mean when you yell an order at me, I should run to do it? What are you running here, a boot camp for priests? I already got out of the boot camp for priests and I will not be one of your stooges. I came here to be a priest and to do priestly duties, I'm not here to jump to your commands. Do you understand?"

"How dare you talk to me like that? I'll fix you! I'm calling Bishop Manning immediately; he'll fix you and he'll fix you good. You will never, ever, talk to a superior in the way you just did every again. I'll have you drummed out of the priesthood, if you ever talk to me or anyone else like that again."

I replied, "Go ahead and call him. It's you that is the impolite priest. The way you've talked to me and Agnes, you should be ashamed of yourself."

The esteem Father Wiggins turned and walked back into his office. I could hear his loud voice screaming into the phone. After a few minutes I could hear him say, "Yes, your Excellency, I understand completely. I'm so sorry. Yes sir, I'll put him right on the phone."

The next thing I knew Father Wiggins was inviting me into his luxurious office. It was five to ten times larger than my bedroom. He handed me the phone and the Bishop said, "Please close the door Father Mitch, I don't want anyone but you to hear what I have to say."

I walked over to where Wiggins was standing and said, "Excuse me Father, but the Bishop wants to speak to me in private." After Wiggins left the room I said, "What's up?"

"Mitch, do you remember what I told you about changing the culture here in this Archdiocese? Some of these old priests think they are God here on earth, but God would never treat people like they do. This Wiggins is one of the worst. If he doesn't change, I'll have to send him into retirement. I've been told he has been like that since he became a priest. I sent you there on purpose. I want you to tell me how things are being run there. We have lots of missing funds and lots of complaints from parishioners there. He's not treating other priests very well, as you could see immediately. It must end. Don't take any of his guff, and you have my approval to talk back to him and refuse to do his bidding. If he tells you to do anything against your standards, refuse. You have my number, make sure you keep in touch with me. And by the way, Agnes called me before Father Wiggins did. She told me your new name, Father Mitch, I like it. Take care and turn things around there."

I hung up the phone and was stunned to say the least. Bishop Manning was going to change culture in the Archdioceses and he's starting here. I'm sure Wiggins will be the perfect gentleman when I open the door. I laughed at the thought. I slowly opened the door and he was standing right there.

Wiggins asked, "Well, what did our young Bishop have to say to you?"

"He asked me to do as you say since you're my boss. Other than that, he thought you must be under some stress to act the way you did. He said he thought you'd apologize as soon as you got me alone."

Wiggins said, "That will never happen! You seem to forget, I'm the boss around here, and don't forget it, understand?"

I pimped him a little bit more, I said, "I thought God was the boss around here, am I wrong?"

"Shut that hole in your face or I'll call the Bishop and ask that he transfer you immediately."

I replied, "Father Wiggins, I asked our Bishop for a transfer immediately and he said I will remain here. He said there are lots of issues here in St. Clement that need to be addressed and he wants me to be vigilant to what goes on here."

Wiggins had a worried look on his face, he quietly replied, "What kind of issues?

"I'm not to speak to you regarding these matters, you'll have to ask the Bishop yourself." Boy did I scare him. I did lie a little, but I'll ask God to forgive me later today.

I went to my room and unpacked my suitcase. I was saying my prayers two hours later when there was a faint knock on my door. I opened the door and there stood Father Wiggins. He said, "I called the Bishop back and he said are no issues that he is worrying about. He also said you made that all up and if you do something like that again you'll be sent to a monastery. You'll do exactly what I say, and I want no lip from you. I run this place and you will respect me and what I tell you to do. Understand?"

"Yeah, I understand. You are the boss. Thank you for explaining everything in such detail." As this jerk walked away the thought crossed my mind, 'Did he really call the Bishop back? Did Bishop Manning not back me up? I can't call him again so soon, can I? I'd best leave well enough alone. I can do this, I can get along with this pompous fool, can't I?'

PRIESTLY DUTIES

I was set up with schedules for consulting and for mass service by the parish secretary Doris. Doris was a woman of about thirty-five. She was married and had two children. She was a salaried employee and was also the accountant for the parish. I was scheduled for my very first counseling session with a married couple by the last name of Davis. The Davis couple were having an issue of getting pregnant. Mr. Davis blamed his wife for her sterilization, but the doctors claimed she was fertile, and it must be Mr. Davis that was sterile or impotent.

I opened my first counseling session with, "I understand that you do not have the ability to bear children, is that correct Mrs. Davis?"

"Call me Betty, Father Mitch. Yes, one of us maybe sterile and it's not me. I've been tested and I'm fertile, but Mr. Davis here won't allow testing. He claims it's me, for he's too much of a man to be sterile."

"What do you say Mr. Davis?"

Davis retorted, "I'm not sterile, it's her. I got a chick pregnant when I was in high school and she lost the kid. You know a miscarriage. So, I know it's not me."

"Mr. Davis, what do you have to lose by getting tested? Maybe the young woman you thought you got pregnant was pregnant by some other guy. That is a possibility, isn't it?"

"No! She was my girl and she didn't mess around; I know that for a fact."

"The only way I can help you two is if you both get tested. Betty, you should have it done again and Mr. Davis you should get tested too.

This blaming each other will get you nowhere. If one of you is sterile you can always adopt."

Mr. Davis stood up and said, "It ain't gonna happen. I'm not sterile. And adopting a kid, are you nuts? Adopted kids never turn out."

I was seeing stars, I yelled back, "They don't turn out? Where did you get that fact, the same place where you believe you're not sterile? I was being polite when I said Betty should be checked again. Sorry to say, but that thinking you got someone pregnant in high school is very inconclusive, meaning there is no proof you were the daddy. More than likely she was having sex with several boys at the same time."

Davis started to walk out the door, he turned back and faced me and said, "I'm going to report you. You don't know what you're talking about. Nancy loved me and she wouldn't have had sex with anyone else."

I responded, "Davis, you are one ignorant man. Your little Nancy had sex with others. Where is she now? Did she have to get married? I'm just guessing she did. Now you can report me to anyone you'd like, but it's you that is wrong here."

Davis stormed out of the office as Betty just sat there. She finally said after he was out of hearing range, "Nancy was the whore of the school. She got knocked up again in her senior year. She had already dropped my husband like a hot potato. I'm sure it was the same guy that knocked her up the first time. My husband was really in love with her. She's been married and divorced now twice and has had three kids."

"Betty, I'm so sorry I was of no help to you and your husband. I guess I'm just not very good at this yet. Your husband is a fool for not hanging onto you."

"Yeah, he is a fool, but this is my last effort trying to save our marriage. Thanks for your help Father Mitch, but this turned out the way I thought it would."

My next counseling session was with a young woman named Callie who was nineteen years old. Callie was living with her father and he had impregnated her. She was raped by him many times over the last four years, because she had no place to go and no place to live. Her mom had passed away several years ago and after her death the father went after her. She wanted to know if the Church would allow her to have an abortion. My personal feelings were yes, go ahead and have this rapist's child aborted. However, it was against the teaching of the Church. I realized this was a very big dilemma for me, since I knew that this baby could be deformed and mentally challenged. Also, the stigma of having one's own father's baby. She cried and cried while telling me her story. I was sick to my stomach when she completed her tale.

I said, "Callie, if you were able to have the child aborted, where would you have this done? I realize that abortion is no longer against the law. Have you seen a doctor?"

Callie sat straight in her chair, and was quite definite I might add, when she said, "I went to a clinic that performs abortions. I don't want this freak of a child and I want my father to go to jail for raping me, that's what I want."

"Callie, as you probably know the Catholic Church is against abortion even though it is now legal. With that being said, I cannot tell you to go ahead and have an abortion. The Church would prefer that you have the baby and just give it up for adoption."

"Is that the best advice you can give me? Why won't you support my decision to abort it? Why don't you tell me it's alright? I want to hear that from you and when it's aborted, I want you to have God forgive me for aborting it."

"Callie, I really feel sorry for you and the predicament you're in. I will tell you this, if you abort the baby, I will gladly give you absolution in the confessional for the sin of the abortion. You can count on that."

"Father Mitch you're a wonderful priest. Thank you for this. Could you also help me get a hold of the police?"

"I'll do what I can, but I can't help you very much on that front. I will make a call on your behalf."

"Please don't tell anyone about this except the cops."

"I cannot say anything unless you ask me too. I do know a cop that may be able to help you out. I call him this afternoon."

I hadn't talked to the cop that had arrested me on my college graduation day, but I kept his phone number. I made the call on Callie's behalf to Ted Boran a St. Paul cop. I explained who I was, and he remembered me. I told him about Callie's dilemma, and I gave him her contact information. He promised me he would see her that day. He also told me he would keep me in the loop about the arrest of her father.

My next counseling session came two days later. The couple was Roger and Beth Young. They were referred to St. Clement by Beth's mother June Dylan. After they sat down, I asked, "I'm not sure why you folks are here, could you please explain your issue?"

Roger was the first to speak, "The reason we're here is because there is no cost in getting counseling at this church. My mother-in-law June Dylan made this appointment for us. I have been unemployed for six months. I was laid off of my construction job and I cannot find other employment. You probably are unaware of this, but there is a recession going on here in Minneapolis and there are no jobs. June thinks I'm lazy. This is the first time in my life I haven't had a job. I'm out every day looking for a job, I'll take anything. Our unemployment insurance has run out and we are going to lose our house. We don't have enough money for food."

Beth then said, "My mother is so selfish. They have the money to help us out, but she refuses. She thinks I should leave Roger and take the kids and move in with them. That is not going to happen! I love Roger and he loves me. Mom wanted us to see a marriage counselor at the cost of twenty dollars a visit. Now where in God's name would we get twenty dollars? If we had that kind of money, we'd buy food."

I was confused. Why were they here? I don't have any money to give them. They're here because I don't charge for counseling. I had no idea what to say to them. The problem they have is financial not spiritual. However, they left me no choice, I had to attempt to help them, I said, "This is a little out of my area of expertise. Your issue is not spiritual. If you have a few sessions here with me, will June then help you out?"

Roger replied, "I have no clue what she will do. Our issue is not with our marriage, it all about money. We will soon be destitute. We have two kids and they are happy little ones. They have no idea what Beth and I are going through."

I said, "Look, I'll try and find some of the Catholic charities that maybe of some help to you. Can you give me a couple of days?"

Roger spoke, "No, we can't. We have no food in the house. June is trying to break us up and she won't help, we have no other place to go."

"How about your folks?"

"Both are dead, I won't go into details."

I reached into my wallet and took out the last bit of money I had to my name, a ten-dollar bill. I handed it to Roger and said, "Will this help until I can try and figure some way to help you out on a more permanent basis?"

Beth spoke up, "Is this coming out of your own money? If it is, we can't take it."

"Beth, you need it more than I do. I get paid at the end of the month and I get fed here for free. Please take it and as I said, I'll try to find something more permanent."

Roger took my ten spot and they both thanked me. I told them I'd call them as soon as I could figure something out.

After the Young's had left, I went to see Father Wiggins. I found him filling his face with a hamburger made by Agnes. I sat down beside him and said, "Father, where do we keep the funds for needy families around here?"

Father replied, "There is no such thing as needy families in our parish. Who's asking?"

"A couple that were referred to me with the last name of Young. A parishioner by the name of June Dylan referred them to us."

"June and her husband Ed are major donors here in the parish and they don't like the kid their daughter married one bit. He's a loser.

They want her to get an annulment so she can marry a man more appropriate for the family. So, we will not help them in any way, do you understand?"

I was shocked, I replied, "What? You won't help them because a large donor in this church wants them to get a divorce? Isn't divorce against everything we hold dear in the Catholic faith?"

"I said annulment, not divorce. And when the man has been unfaithful to the woman an annulment is the only answer. June knows as a fact he's fooled around."

"So what? Does that concern us, or June for that matter? Doesn't it just concern the Young's. Please Father, these kids need some financial help and they need it now."

"No! They will get no help from us or from the Dylan's."

"Well, I don't care what you say, I'm going to find them some help, if I have to personally do it myself."

"You do that, and I'll have you transferred out of here tomorrow. If I do that, no other church will touch you. Stay out of things that don't concern you."

"I took a vow to help people in need and I won't let you bully me into not helping the needy. What is wrong with you, has a little power gone to your head?"

"You heard me, now get out of here, I want to finish my lunch."

I walked out of the parish house and strolled towards a small shopping center a few blocks away. I found a payphone and inserted my dime. I dialed the Bishop's phone number and his receptionist answered. I asked for the Bishop and she put me on hold. A few minutes later the Bishop answered and said, "Hello Father Mitch, is this about Father Wiggins?"

I replied, "Yes, it is. I'm so sorry to bother you but this can't wait."

Bishop Manning quietly said, "Mitch, I personally made your first assignment St. Clement. I did that for a reason. I wanted you to learn how to adjust and how to learn our system. You must figure out a way to help these people without the help of Father Wiggins. He's not going to help you. If you are to be a successful counselor, you must find ways to help your parishioners in need by yourself. I'm not going to abandon you, but I want you to learn how to fend for yourself."

"Did Wiggins tell you anything about what's going on here?"

"Yes, he did, he called me a few minutes ago. I'm sure I did not get the whole story or a truthful story. Let the sleeping dog lie for now. Find a way to help this couple out yourself, I have confidence in you, and I know you'll figure this out."

"Alright then, I'll figure it out."

CHARITABLE WORKS & HAM DINNER

I stood for a long while by that phone booth trying to come up with a plan. It dawned on me that this whole neighborhood was where our parishioners lived. Why not contact them for help? I went back to the rectory and asked Agnes if I could have a list of all the businesses that were members of our congregation. It took her two minutes to find what I wanted. She said, "Father Wiggins calls these folks all the time for money."

First on the list was a fellow named Larry Sondrall who owned a pretty large food mart down the street. I walked to Larry's store and I found him in his office. I introduced myself. I asked, "Larry, I know you have donated funds to our church, but I was wondering if you would donate food to a needy family? They're pretty destitute at the present time and food is their number one need."

Larry looked cautiously at me and said, "Is this a onetime deal or are you going to hit me up every day? If it's an everyday thing the answer is no? Wiggins thinks I made of money, but I'm not. I'm sick of that guy always asking just a few of us for money."

"I promise you that it will not be an everyday thing. But what I was thinking, is maybe you could run a tab and let them buy food on credit. When Roger gets a job, they could start paying you back."

"What's this Roger's background? By background, I mean what kind of work did he do?"

"I believe he was in construction. And, in full disclosure, his wife, Beth's mother is Mrs. Dylan. I think you may know her."

Larry stared at me without blinking an eye and said, "I'll do whatever I can to help those kids out. You have Roger and his wife come and see me this afternoon, I have an idea that may work out for the both of them and for me. I'd like you there too. How about one o'clock?"

I said, "I'll be back here at one with Roger and Beth. Thanks Larry, you're the best."

At one o'clock, Roger, Beth and I walked into the Shoppers Mart Grocery in south Minneapolis. Larry was standing in his office with another man as we walked in. Larry waved us back and quickly introduced us to a fellow name Tony Keller. Larry explained to Roger that Tony owned a hardware store on the same block as Larry's store.

Tony said, "Roger, I need a man that can install appliances such as washer, dryers, water heaters, water softeners as well as other plumbing problems. I can teach you most of the plumbing issues and hopefully you know how to install the appliances. The pay is six-fifty an hour with two weeks' vacation. If you take my offer, I'll give you two weeks advance on your salary to help you get caught up on some of your bills. I expect you to work hard and be polite to all the customers. When not on an installation call you must work in the store helping customers."

Roger had tears in his eyes, he said, "Mr. Keller, I accept your offer and I will work my tail off for you. I cannot thank you enough."

Keller replied, "I'm not done yet. And you Beth, I'd like you to work part time in the store too, helping customers and doing some small book work. The pay is five bucks and hour. Whaddya think?"

"I think you just hired two people. This is the best day of our married life. You guys are the best."

Larry then interjected, "Also, I have six bags of groceries ready for you to take home. There is no charge the food. In addition, I've set up a charge account for you here at the store. You can buy your food and pay off the bill when you get paid."

I looked at Roger and Beth and they were both crying. "Beth tearfully said, "We don't know how to thank you guys. And you Father

Mitch, I can't believe you could do all of this for us. You are truly a representative of God; you are a miracle worker."

I finally said, "It wasn't me; it was Larry and Tony here that are the miracle workers. Thanks to both of you."

After we filled up the Young's car, they dropped me off at the rectory. I walked in and Father Wiggins said, "Where have you been? We had to postpone our one o'clock meeting because we couldn't find you. Where have you been?"

"I was helping the Young family get new jobs and food. I must admit it went very well."

"You went against my wishes and helped those two out."

"I didn't go against your wishes at all, I just didn't ask Mrs. Dylan for any help. I found my own help."

"Just who helped you out?"

I wasn't sure I wanted to divulge my sources, but I also figured I'd better come clean. I replied, "Larry Sondrall and Tony Keller. They were happy to help those kids out."

"I thought I told you to stay away from our big donors?"

"To be honest with you, I didn't realize that they were big donors. They were just happy to help. Tony was looking for someone to install appliances and Roger filled in his search nicely. He also hired Beth. It worked out for everyone."

Father Wiggins yelled, "I have rescheduled the meeting for five, make sure you're there."

I replied, "Yes Sir!" I then saluted him like I was in the army. His face turned red and he walked away.

The meeting took place in Father Wiggins office. As I stated before it was a wonderful, very large, opulent office with elegant furnishings. It's the type of opulence you'd find in the office of a CEO of a large corporation, but not in the office of a lowly pastor. Father was sitting behind the largest desk I had ever seen. There was only one sheet of paper on the desk. He started with, "Since you all know one another here, we can begin without delay."

I raised my hand in the air and said, "Forgive me Father, but you are the only one I know here."

Father took a deep breath and said, "Alright then. This is Mr. Graves; he heads up the committee for the ham dinner. He will report to you. Also, to my left is Father Cole, to the left of him is Father Basil, both are assistants here at St. Clement."

I stood up and said, "It's a pleasure to meet both of you. I've seen you both around, but we've never talked." I also said hello to Mr. Graves, and I shook all their hands and sat immediately down.

Wiggins said, "Sitting on your chairs was the itinerary for the ham dinner. We will follow it to the letter. Father Collins, this is your responsibility and I expect you to keep in mind that this is the biggest fundraiser we have here at St. Clement. Don't mess this up!"

"You are all dismissed. You may finish this meeting without me in the basement offices. Thank you all."

After we got down to the basement dungeon Mr. Graves said, "Listen, this will be my last year doing this. I just don't have time any longer. In fact, I'll only be able to help out on a limited basis. I told Father that I didn't want to do it this year, but he insisted."

I smiled at Mr. Graves and said, "I think I understand your reluctance to working on this project. Father Wiggins can be difficult to work with."

Father Basil quickly replied, "I'd watch what I'm saying about our esteemed pastor. He's a great man and a wonderful priest. He has taken this parish out of poverty and made it a solid church financially."

I snidely said, "Yeah, he's made the church profitable, but are the souls here rich in their religion? I'm guessing they have issues with him, I know I do."

Basil replied, "I refuse to work with a snot nosed kid like you. You've been a priest for a couple of months, and you talk that way? Goodbye Mr. Collins. Did you notice I didn't say Father Collins, it's because I suspect you won't be a priest very long?"

Father Cole said, "I'm out of here too. I just don't need this crap from some young kid."

Mr. Graves looked at the two of them and said, "I'm staying. I'm happy you two pompous asses are leaving. You should take Wiggins with you and all of you leave our parish. I hope you two idiots realize that the parishioners in this church are fed up with you two and the pastor as well. So, get your fat asses out here right now, Father Mitch and I have work to do. And, hurry now, go tell your daddy, papa Wiggins, that mean old Gary Graves was so mean to you. Out! Get out now!"

The two priests moved quickly out of the room and Gary laughed and said, "Now we can get some work done. The last couple of years has been hell around here with this stupid ham dinner. It's been a bust for the last five years and the only reason Wiggins can claim it's successful is everything is donated. We've wanted to have games both indoors and outdoors but that has always been shot down. I'm hoping you'll see it our way and change this whole thing around."

I said, "Yes, I like the idea of games. We can have a dunk tank and I'll be the person that gets dunked. Also, we can a basketball shooting contest for prizes. How about a roulette wheel with prizes in that too? There are all kinds of games we can use. This will be fun."

"Do you mind if I call you Father Mitch?"

"I prefer you call me just Mitch, especially when it's just the people working on the dinner."

"Mitch, I know so many folks that would want to help out and take this ham dinner back to what it once was. It was fun and all of the members of the congregation got to know one another through this dinner and helping out to make it successful. I'll make some calls and we'll be overwhelmed with help. Can we move the meeting to the school?"

"We can and we will. You make some calls and if you can give me some numbers, I'll make some of the calls too."

I got some more good news later that day, when Officer Ted Boran called me. He said, "Father Mitch, we got that bastard that was raping Callie. Oops, sorry Father about the bad language. But we got him. We brought him in and interrogated him for three hours before he confessed. He wanted to see her and apologize, but she wouldn't see him. This clown will do some serious time. He raped her when she was fifteen years old. That's statutory rape. That poor kid. Thanks for tipping us off about this ass. Oops, sorry again Father about my bad language. I used some of my old arithmetic skills and I think he might get ten to fifteen years in the pen."

I laughed and replied, "Ted, I'm used to that kind of language but arithmetic skills, you're getting old? I haven't heard that word used in a long while. I have heard the other words used and I used them myself. I'm a priest but I did live in the real world at one time in my life. Thanks for helping Callie out. When you see her, ask her to come and see me. By the way, what's her last name?"

"I'll tell her you want to see her, and her last name is Gavrilo. And, thanks for tipping us off about the old man."

CALLIE GAVRILO

I received a call two weeks after Callie's father was picked up the charges of rape. She asked me if she could come back for a counseling session. I told her I was worried about her and, and yes, she could come in anytime.

Two days later Callie and I met in one of the small offices in the rectory basement. She looked happy as she wore a big grin on her face. I asked her, "How are you doing, you look happy?"

She said, "I'm happy enough. But, Father Mitch, I need to get something off my chest, however; my father confessed a long time ago that he killed my mom. It was about two years ago; I went into his bedroom with a butcher knife and I was intent on killing him. He woke and beat the crap out of me. All the while he screamed, 'I killed your damn mother and if you want, I'll kill you too! She wouldn't give me sex and you better, or you'll be dead right along with her.' He then raped me. I called Mr. Boran back and told him about my mother's death and he said he'd look into it. They interrogated my father for a few hours, and he finally confessed to that too. After Mr. Boran told him he'd likely do life in prison, he turned his house over to me as well as the insurance money he got for my mom's death. It was twenty-five thousand dollars. He wrote me a letter apologizing for what he'd done to me and Mom. And, I also had an abortion."

I sat back and tried to digest all she had told me. The abortion part was the only thing I didn't know how to respond to. "Do you want absolution? I'd happily give it to you. I know if you're sorry, God will forgive you."

"Can I go to confession in the church? I'd like that very much. You see, Dad wouldn't let me go to church after he started having his way with me. He called me a sinful slut."

"When do you want to go?"

"How about right now?"

Callie and I walked to the church and entered the confessional. Callie knelt down and I opened the curtain to the confessional. She said, "Bless me Father for I have sinned, I killed my baby. I also hated my father for what he did to me, and I can't forgive him for that."

I smiled to myself, and thought, 'I hate that bastard too, so don't feel all alone Callie.' However, I said, "Callie, your sins are forgiven, please go out and find some happiness in your life. For your penance do some acts of charity."

"Thank you, Father Mitch, but what acts of charity can I do?"

"I haven't given that any thought. Well, there is something you could do for me. Would you consider working with me and a few other parishioners on the yearly ham dinner. It's a big event here at St. Clement and support has been dwindling for several years now."

"I'd love to help out. Getting out and meeting people will do me some good. When do I start and what time should I be here and what do you want me to do?"

"We have a meeting tonight at the school around seven. We now have five of us working on the dinner, which will take place in three weeks. We'll go over everything tonight."

"I'll be there."

At promptly seven o'clock, Callie Gavrilo, Larry Sondrall, Gary Graves, Tony Keller and I, all sat down to discuss the ham dinner after all the introductions were made. I directed my first comments to Callie, I asked, "Callie, would you mind going around to the businesses that are owned or run by parishioners and asked for their support? By support I mean financial support or donations of gifts for our games.

We could use just about anything that is new and has not been used as gifts."

Callie responded, "Wow! I didn't expect that. I guess that would get me out of my sheltered existence. I'll do it, just give me the names and addresses."

After talking about all the issues, we needed to discuss, Tony Keller said, "I think we need more folks to help out. Callie in your attempt to get donations, if someone says they cannot afford to contribute anything, will you ask them to help out by working at our event? That way we can encourage all of our parishioners to be involved. And Father Mitch, can you speak at all the masses and encourage all the parishioners to get involved?"

"Yes sir, Mr. Keller, I'll do as you asked." I saluted Tony in a military way and the entire group laughed hysterically as we adjourned the meeting.

Callie began her workload early the next morning and I went along with her. I did so because I knew only of few of the parishioners myself. I realized then that Callie was a beautiful young woman with a wonderful personality. The first business we entered was a Mom and Pop small grocery store down the block from the church. Callie introduced me and she went to work on them. They didn't have much money, but they were about to donate ten dollars when Callie said, "Wait a minute. Why don't you keep your money and just help us out at the dinner? We could use your help more than your money."

Both of them smiled and said they would attend the next meeting.

The entire day went the same way. Whenever a parishioner had nothing to contribute, Callie asked them to help out at the dinner. Not one refused to help. It was a wonderful day for me as well as for Callie. I met so many people I had to make a list of all their names. Callie had collected over fifteen hundred dollars in cash and checks and also had commitments for new goods to be used as gift for the games. Many donated and also committed to help out at the dinner. We had so many commitments from people to help out, I thought we'd have more volunteers than diners. Callie laughed at my comments and just shook her head at me. I had a great day and it was mostly because of watching this young woman mesmerize all of these parishioners with her wonderful, outgoing, confident personality. She indeed will not let her past interfere with her future. She is someone special.

The last place we stopped was Jerry's Garage, a very large auto repair business. Jerry was out but his son David Clough was there, and he invited us into the office. After we sat down Callie went to work on young David. Now when I say young, he looked like he was about sixteen, but he informed me that he was twenty-two. He stared at Callie and smiled at everything she said. She finally said, "Are you mimicking me or making fun of me? If so, please stop or we'll leave."

David stuttered, "Oh no! I... wasn't making... fun or mimicking you. I was enjoying watching you. You are the prettiest, nicest girl I've ever seen. Please don't go. Please, I just want to get to know you better."

Callie calmly said, "No you don't. You wouldn't like me if you knew my past."

I just sat back watching the two of them. Callie was determined not to tell David about her past and David was not going to let her leave him hanging there. He said, "I don't care a rat's behind about your past, I want to know about the future. Please let me get to know you better. This is the first time in my life I've been so forward. I'm pretty shy but around you I'm not. I'll get my dad to donate a couple of oil changes and a hundred bucks too."

Callie replied, "Thank you David. Would you also like to help out and be on our committee? We meet three times a week at the school for a couple of hours."

"If you're going to be there I'll be there. I'll bring my dad along too."

Callie replied, "Alright then. I'll meet you and Dad at the school at seven tomorrow night."

We walked out of the auto shop and strolled down the street. I said, "That went very well, don't you think?"

Callie smiled at me and said, "You're a sly old fox. You didn't say a word, you wanted me to fend for myself. How did I do?"

"You did better than I expected. Listen Callie, you have a gift when it comes to talking to people. Your personality resonates confidence. For a young woman that has endured all that you have, you are clearly not going to let it define you. David likes you, and he doesn't need to know what happened to you. At some point if you two like one another a lot, you can tell him what you lived through. His reaction will define your future with him. He seemed like a good guy, only time will tell if he's right for you."

"Wow! Thanks for all the kind words, but I don't think I deserve them. I do like him though. I've never had a boyfriend before; I think it would be really nice."

"Let's get you home. By the way where do you live and now that the house is yours, what will you do with it?"

"I've already listed it with a broker. I'm not living there now. I'm staying in a motel. I just can't go back there, too many bad memories."

"How would you like me to get you a better place to live. Our housekeeper Agnes is looking for someone to stay with her. She's all alone and I think you two would hit it off. What do you say?"

"I say okay. But Father Mitch, will she know about my past? My God, what will I do? People will want to know and I'm not sure I'm strong enough to advertise it to everyone I meet."

"Callie, you don't need to tell anyone unless you want too. You did nothing wrong. This is something you can share if you want to get it off your chest."

Callie smiled again at me and said, "You make me feel so good about myself, thank you Father Mitch for being my friend. I never thought a priest could be so nice. The rest of those guys at St. Clement are not like you."

I replied, "Everyone is different, and those guys are different. See you tomorrow at the school."

PREPARATIONS FOR THE HAM DINNER

At seven o'clock the next evening I walked over to the school and the parking lot was full. When I say full, I mean they were parking on the street. I went downstairs to the lunchroom and there were so many people I couldn't count them all. Callie and David walked up to me and said at the same time, "Father Mitch, we did it." They both laughed at saying the exact same words. Callie quickly said, "Great minds think alike, don't they?"

I said, "What did you kids do to get all these people here?"

David smiled and said, "Callie and I got together last night and called everyone. The reception we got was overwhelming. More people offered us cash, and all promised to work at the dinner."

Callie grabbed my arm and walked me away from the others and said, "Father Mitch, I've got about fifteen thousand dollars in cash and checks. David and I went around all of today and saw all the people that pledged last night. I'm scared, what do I do with all this money?"

"This is unbelievable. You two kids raised all that money? In the last couple of years, records show they only netted around seven thousand after expenses. I wonder where all that money went?"

Callie said, "Should I give the money to Mr. Sondrall and Mr. Keller to hold for us?"

"That's a good idea. It would be in good hands with those two. Callie you are a wonder worker. I've can't believe you and David did all of this. Did you tell him anything?"

"I did and he cried. So, did I. I also told Agnes. She cried too. I wanted both of them to know who they were spending time with. So, I confessed, and the reception couldn't have been better. I moved in with Agnes yesterday. I have my own room and she wants me to stay until I graduate from college or even longer. I'm getting signed up for the U of M tomorrow. I'm going to be a teacher."

I laughingly said, "I thought you were going to take auto mechanics."

Callie and I walked back to where all the volunteers were waiting, and Larry took over with Tony right beside him. My friend Gary Graves had put them in charge of the kitchen and the food preparations. Larry would order all the precooked hams, potatoes and gravy, veggies and desserts from his store at cost. He had several men and women that worked in restaurants around the parish that volunteered to be the cooks. Tony ran the set up in the dining area and Gary would be in charge of the games. Callie would help me with all the paperwork.

I asked all of the volunteers to invite all their friends and relatives as I was going to do. I called Kit and told her about the dinner, and she said Mom and Bud would come along with her and Mike. The last person I called was Bishop Manning. I asked if he could come and he was hesitant to make a commitment. He said, "Mitch, if I came to your dinner, then all the parishes would want me to attend theirs. I'm not sure I can do this. Sorry."

I said, "I understand completely but there is something I want you to know. Before this event takes place, we have raised over fifteen thousand dollars. That is a fundraising miracle. Bishop, in the last few years, after expenses the parish showed a profit of only seven thousand. I predict we make somewhere around thirty to forty thousand if no one gets their hands on that cash, the whole community of this church wants to be involved in this fundraising effort. I've never realized that we'd get such a turn out to help with this dinner."

Bishop Manning said quickly after I gave him the potential profits, "I'll be there. Please don't tell Father Wiggins, okay?"

The volunteers had everything ready for the famous ham dinner. All of the games were set up in the gym except the dunk tank, which was set up behind the school. Several of the men volunteered to be the first target to be dropped in the tank should someone hit the bullseye with a baseball. I had volunteered to be there at two o'clock sharp to take my turn. There was a big crowd expected to see me go into the tank. None of the other priest volunteered for this duty.

My mom, Bud, Kit and Mike all showed up and I was excited to see all of them. I introduced Callie and David to them as we sat down near the main table in the lunchroom. There were name tags placed at each one of the twenty place settings on the main table and they did not include any priests. I specifically told Tony and Larry I wanted volunteers seated at the head table not priests. When Father Wiggins walked in followed by fathers Basil and Cole, they all looked for their name tags on the head table. Wiggins asked Tony, "Where am I supposed to sit? Certainly not at a table with all the parishioners, am I?"

Tony laughed and said, "Yes, you are going to sit with all of us common folks, if you want to eat. You three will sit off to left at that table with those families. Enjoy."

Father Wiggins was upset, and he began walking straight towards me. I figured he'd try and slug me if I wasn't careful. Just before he reached me, I saw Bishop Manning approaching me. Wiggins got to me first, without knowing the Bishop was right behind him, he choked back the words, "Are you insane? You've left us off the main table. Just who do you think runs this place, and it isn't you? I'll make sure you never work at another parish as long as you live."

I quietly said, "Father, all these parishioners have volunteered their time, money and expertise on getting this large turnout for the dinner. I thought it should be them that are honored, don't you?"

"No, I don't! It's the priest that should be honored for all the work they do, not a bunch of commoners."

Bishop Manning tapped Wiggins on the shoulder and Wiggins turned and was about to attack whomever it was that touched him.

He was surprised, or I should say stunned, and was lost for words. Manning said, "Would you mind if I sat with you and the other priests. This is quite an event; wouldn't you say so Father Wiggins?"

"Yes, quite an event. We've worked so hard on this year's dinner and we were able to get several new people to volunteer."

Manning continued to pimp him, "Well Father, what's your guess on the revenue associated with this event?"

"Early indication are around seven thousand dollars, give or take a few hundred. It should be a good take."

"How much have you grossed in years past?"

"Right around that seven thousand number."

"Did you have a hand in putting the dinner together? It seems like a lot of work."

"Yes, lots of work but we got it done. I spearheaded the whole thing with the help of Father Cole and Father Basil."

"Did Father Mitch help out at all.?"

"Yes, he had a small part in putting it together."

"That's good, let us find our seats and listen to the program."

Tony Keller was the first to speak, he began, "Our famous ham dinner was almost done in, until Father Mitch came along. With him guiding all of us we raised a record amount of funds to help the homeless in our parish. It will also help fund the deficits that our school is running. So, Father Mitch, hats off to you."

Everyone stood and clapped and cheered for me. They screamed for me to stand up, which I did. I waved with a slight tear running down my cheek. Tony asked me to speak so I said, "I'd like to thank all of you that helped make this dinner so successful. There are just too many of you to name individually so thank you one and all. There is one person I want to mention however, it is Callie Gavrilo. Callie asked me what she could do to help our parish out and I asked her to raise some money and awareness of our ham dinner. Callie took charge and she, with the help of David Clough, raised over fifteen thousand dollars in one day. That is also the power of our community giving to our church. This dinner should bring approximately thirty to forty thousand dollars into the church's coffers. And, it was done by the efforts of all of you. Thank you all so much. Now, I'd like to introduce to you our Bishop Manning, who came here to see the how he can take what we've done here and show other church's that they can do it too. Bishop Manning folks."

The Bishop stood up and said, "Thank you all for inviting me to this wonderful dinner. Father Mitch is something special, isn't he? As Father said, we will try and duplicate what you folks did here and try it elsewhere."

The Bishop sat down next to Wiggins and said, "So, seven thousand dollars? Where did the other twenty-five thousand or so go to? Did you buy another new car this year Father? I am going to do an audit of this church for the last five years and if I find there are some indiscretions, I'll go back to the first year you were here, understand?"

Wiggins quietly said, "Of course Bishop, of course."

AFTER THE DINNER

After we finished our dinners, my family followed me out to the back of the church. I had changed into a tee shirt and a swimsuit and I could hear all the snickering going on behind my back. I reached the chair to the tank and waited for the first customer. It was then I looked at the line waiting to dunk me. It had snaked around the school and I thought it looked like a hundred people in the line. I was in for a wet afternoon. I smiled and looked at the first person in line. It was Tony Keller and he was ready for me. He went into a windup and the ball spun off the water and hit me in the leg. Tony yelled, "Father Mitch are you all right?"

I yelled back, "Come on Tony, you can do better than that."

He did, the next ball hit the target and I was dumped into five feet of water. I jumped up and said, "We better move that counter back about fifty-feet, this distance is too easy." The crowd roared and the game became more fun. I must have been dunked more than twenty-five times and it was so much fun.

I was given a towel by Callie and I saw she had tears running down her face from laughing so much. David introduced me to his family. His father Jerry said, "It's so nice to finally meet a good priest around here. If there anything I can do for you, don't hesitate to ask."

I replied, "Jerry there is something you could help me with. I need a car. An old car, but one in good condition. Something around one hundred bucks, if possible."

Jerry was laughing as hard as Callie had been. Jerry smiled at me and said, "A hundred bucks? I can get you a bicycle for a hundred bucks."

I replied, "Oh, I see, that's not possible any longer. Well, forget it for now, I'll just have to wait until my ship comes in. That's the correct term, isn't it?"

Jerry said, "I don't know about terms. Come and see me Monday and I'll have a suitable vehicle for you, at no charge. It's the least I can do for helping my son get out of his shell. And, that little Callie, what a wonderful young lady. See you Monday morning."

In the late evening I heard a soft rap on my door. I opened the door to my closet sized room and there was Father Wiggins standing there. He asked, "Could you please come down to my office, please?"

He said please twice. I was experiencing a miracle, a miracle I tell you. Wiggins was a broken man, at least that's what it appeared to be. I replied, "Why yes Father." I followed him down the stairs and into his opulent office. I could hardly wait for his confession and apology for all the things he had done to disrupt the dinner preparations.

He sat down behind his desk and said, "What have I done to have you cause me all this trouble? We were doing just fine here at St. Clement before you came here and disrupted everything I've built. You should be ashamed, but you're not. I see that you take pride in causing mayhem in our good little parish. From now on, you will not work on any committees, you will only do priestly things, such as; hear confessions, say daily mass and conduct counseling sessions and administer the sacraments. No fundraising of any kind and stay away from our main contributors. I also strongly suggest you spend the rest of your days here at St. Clement in prayer and fasting. You should ask the good Lord for his forgiveness for what you have done to this parish. Now, do you have any questions?"

I was shocked at his comments. I was wondering as he was speaking, if he had talked to Bishop Manning about the differential in his financial outlook on the ham dinner to the actual results. I finally said, "Father Wiggins, are you trying to rein me in? Did I offend you with the success of the dinner? Wasn't clearing more than thirty thousand dollars good for the parish? Just what is your point in this meeting? Are you trying to show me whose boss around here? I do know it's you."

Wiggins replied, "You and I both know whose boss around here and it is me. I'm sick and tired of your interference in our parish culture. I run things the way they should be here at St. Clement and I don't need the help of a young whippersnapper like you telling what to do. I spoke to the Bishop and he agreed with me. If you don't do as I say you'll be transferred out of here immediately. Now, you can run and call our esteem Bishop and ask him to change my mind but he will not even talk to you. I went over his head on this and he has agreed not to speak to you again. Archbishop Ryan is his boss, and he saw what you have done and he sided with me. I did not steal any funds from this church as you suggested. All the funds in the last five years have been accounted for, including this year. Now, get your ass out of my office and stay away from me and Fathers Cole and Basil."

I was stunned to say the least. The Archbishop? My Lord, he went to the Archbishop. He's right, it's impossible to change the culture in these parishes. It's old men running things and they are all buddies from their seminary days and they all stick together. I'm screwed, to say the least.

I said the six o'clock mass the next morning and as usual there were three parishioners in attendance. My sermon was short and sweet, about fifty words. I am down and I am dejected. I thought I was doing so well. The people I brought back to the church are going to hate me. I just can't face them again. What will I do?

I called the Bishop and was told he was busy and he would call me back. I never heard from him. Well, I don't know for sure if he called me back, Wiggins never said I had a call. I was shunned by Wiggins and his two-puppet priests. There was no doubt in my mind that those two so-called priests, wanted to be just like big daddy Wiggins.

So much for unifying the parish. All my work was for naught. I tried to explain my dilemma to the people I had gotten close to such as Tony, Larry and Gary. They all understood and said they would disassociate themselves from St. Clement. They would all find a new parish where they would be welcomed. I told Callie what happened and she said, "I don't care about St. Clement; I care about you. You are like my older brother not my priest. No one has ever done the things that you have done for me. I love you Father Mitch, it's love like I'd feel for a brother, if I had one. I will always be your friend."

I gave Callie a hug and said, "I feel the same way as you. You are the best thing that has come out of my stay here. You promise to keep in touch, don't you?" Callie cried and shook her head yes as she walked away.

NEW LIFE

Nine months had passed since my demotion and I was living like a zombie. My family stayed in touch, especially my sister Kit. My young friend Callie called me daily or stopped by after mass weekly so she could find out how I was doing. God clearly blessed me when He brought Callie into my life. I was not like a brother to her any longer, I was more like her dad. She told me all the things she would tell a mother or a father, not a priest or even a friend. I shared my anger and my disappointment in the Catholic Church with her and she kept telling me to hang in there something good was coming my way. As I thought about her background and what she endured, my problems seem so minuscule. I would try and endure.

We were in the middle of winter and it was a cold March Friday night. I was the only priest that heard confessions on Friday night. The others worked for two hours on Saturday mornings. I was also there on Saturday mornings, but I worked four hours. I was always the stooge that got all the bad duty. The other priests just laughed when I walked by. I never ate with them any longer, always by myself. I was one unhappy priest.

Late one Friday night as I stood up to leave the confessional, someone, whispered, "Am I too late Father?"

I replied, "Of course not. Come in and I'll hear your confession."

The woman began, "Bless me Father for I have sinned, my last confession was around fourteen years ago. Where would you like me to start Father?"

"I have all night, so start wherever you're most comfortable. And believe me, I've heard it all. So please don't think I'll judge you or you won't get absolution, because you will, if you're sorry for your sins. Please begin."

"Father I've done some bad things in my life that I'm ashamed of, and some things that the Church will frown upon but I'm not ashamed of. Does that make sense?"

I laughed at her comments before saying, "We have all done somethings we're not proud of and somethings that we shouldn't have done. However, we wouldn't change them if our lives depended upon it. So, go ahead and continue."

She continued, "I had sex when I was very young, very, very young. It was consensual and I loved the person so much. As I got older, I had sex again in high school several times with two different guys. Now I'm ashamed of that but I'm not ashamed of the first time. After I graduated from college, I got pregnant by my boyfriend. We had a baby girl."

"Did you get married?"

"Yes, right away. When the baby was born, he wanted a divorce. He didn't want to be married any longer, he said things were not going well, so why should he stay. I had insisted originally that we get married by a Justice of the Peace because it was the quickest way. My folks would not come to the wedding or our little reception. In fact, they disowned me after my baby was born. I'm now divorced and I was wondering; first, can I get that marriage annulled, and second, will you give me absolution? Six months after we were married, I insisted that we have the marriage blessed by a Catholic priest, which we did. So, in the eyes of the Church we're married. I'm hoping God will forgive me for the premarital sex and not getting married in the Church originally. But a divorce, from what I remember from school is the church is against divorce and they don't recognize it. I'm so sorry Father to bore you with all these things but I'm very confused, please help me."

I smiled at her last comments, I responded, "You didn't bore me, quite the contrary, you intrigued me. You see I get paid the big bucks to work all these issues out. I hope you know I'm just teasing. Everything you asked can be worked out. Annulment is very expensive. Let me explain my experience with annulments; I had a couple in counseling where the man had been divorced but wanted to become a Catholic. He had been married also by a Justice of the Peace. He agreed to an annulment and I began the paperwork. I told him we needed five hundred dollars up front to begin the process. Several weeks later, I was told we would need another one thousand dollars to complete the annulment, and he was willing to pay that amount too. Another few weeks passed and I was told they would need to pay an additional two thousand dollars to finally get the annulment approved by Rome. The man said no. He told me that his best friend had a similar thing happen to him but in the end, they wanted a total of ten thousand dollars to complete the annulment. That man walked away too. So, that's what you're looking at. My question to you is; are you made of money?"

"No, I'm not. My ex-husband has refused to pay any support for my daughter or me. He now claims she's not his. The reason we split up was he had a girlfriend and had her for quite a while. Unbeknownst to him, she came over to our apartment and asked me to divorce him so they could get married. He had told her I knew about the two of them, which I didn't. After that, I was happy to get rid of him. Oh Father, I'm so sorry for dragging this on so long. Thank you for your patience."

"I will give you absolution immediately and then would you call the parish house and make an appointment for a counseling session. I think I can relieve some of your doubts about the church and I may be able to help you get some financial aid. Okay?"

"Thanks Mitch, I'll get an appointment."

I gave her absolution and something was not right. She said, 'Thanks Mitch.' Now, only a few friends and family called me Mitch. Who was this woman? I wondered if it was Leanne? Kit told me she married and Italian guy and she had two kids. This woman said she has a daughter.

Three days later on a Monday morning, there was a soft knock on the office door in the rectory basement. I said, "Come in the doors open."

The door slowly opened and Sybil Newman said, "Hello Mitch. Oops, I mean Father Mitch. How are you, may I sit down?"

I must have had a pale look on my face as Syb said again, "May I sit down? Are you all right? You look like you may be sick. Did I surprise you?"

I cleared my throat and said, "Surprise? You'll never know how surprised I am. Was it you that came to confession last week?"

Syb lowered her head as I could see she was embarrassed. She quietly said, "Yes, that was me. You must think I'm an old slut. I'm sorry I bothered you Mitch, I bet I'm the last person you wanted to see. I can just go if you'd like."

"Don't you dare walk out on me again. I've wondered what happened to you. You moved away and Kit could never find out where you went. You have a daughter; I hope she looks like you. My goodness girl, you look as young and beautiful as you did when we were kids."

"Thanks Mitch, you look pretty darn good yourself. How's life as a priest?"

"Things could be better, a whole lot better. Do you have to get home anytime soon? If not, let's get out of here so we can talk in private."

"I thought this would be private. Where do you want to go? I don't have to be home until two."

We walked out of the rectory and got into my old jalopy. When Jerry Clough said he'd get me a used car, I didn't think it would be fifteen years old. Believe me when I say, it was better than nothing. Syb stared at my car and said, "Will this thing get us to a coffee shop. If not, I have a car that's about eight or nine years newer."

I replied, "Listen smarty-pants, this car is like new. And the cost was not substantial. It was free. Get in and be quiet."

Syb laughed and said, "Nothing has changed over the last ten plus years, has it?"

We arrived at the coffee shop out of my neighborhood. I had also taken off my priest suit and collar. I looked like a normal guy. Syb sat down and I looked her over. She was beautiful, maybe gorgeous would be a better way to describe her. Her smile drove me nuts. There was nothing that I didn't like about her. As I was undressing her in my mind, the thought that I'm a priest didn't even register. I finally said, "Coffee?"

"I suppose we should have coffee since we're in a coffee house. I want mine black. Do you still have yours with all that cream and sugar like a little girl?" She started laughing and couldn't stop. I laughed along with her as I found her personality mesmerizing. She was so cute. My God, what is happening to me?

I got the coffee and asked, "How long have you been divorced?"

"Let's see. My daughter Sammy is four now, so close to four years. As soon as I got pregnant, he ran off to his old girlfriend's arms."

"I hope you realize in the eyes of the church you are still married. I personally think this annulment thing is a piece of crap. It's no different than a divorce, it dissolves a marriage. The only difference is the church makes money off of it and after they say you were never married. In my mind, when two people can't get along why not dissolve the marriage and let them both move on."

"You don't sound like a priest Mitch. In fact, you sound more like me than a priest."

"Syb, I'm sorry to say, I have some serious doubts about staying in the priesthood. About a year ago I was on top of the world. But after a few weeks of being at St. Clement, I realized the Catholic Church is run by a group of old men that do not want change. It's unfortunate because I thought the new bishop wanted to change the culture here but the higher ups wouldn't allow it."

"You sound pretty bummed out. Is there anything I can do for you?"

"Just be my friend. I need a friend."

WHAT TO DO???

Syb and I sat in that coffee shop for three hours. We ordered lunch and laughed continuously. It was so much fun, much more fun than I had in the last year and it was only in three hours. When we were ready to leave, I said, "What's next? Can we see each other again?"

Syb replied, "I'd like that but… I'm not sure I want to interfere with your life as a priest. I didn't go to confession to get you to leave the priesthood. I came to confession to get absolution from a priest I knew would understand my problems. If you have romantic thoughts about us, I'm sorry but we can't see each other. I just can't do that."

"Syb, I don't know what I want. I do know that I'd like to see you again. Today was one of the best days I've had in a long while. As far as romantic thoughts, I've always had romantic thoughts about you. I just can't help it. Those thoughts got me through the seminary and they've gotten me this far as a priest. It's just that I'm not sure I can keep on living this lie I've lived for the last ten years. Please let me see you and we'll see where things go."

"Nope! I won't be the person that encourages you to leave the priesthood. Besides, I do have a guy friend that I'm seeing. I like him and he likes me. The only issue is that he doesn't like kids. But my little girl Sammy goes with me. It's a package deal and I'm afraid she will be a deal breaker. So, you'll have to find someone else. Mitch, I've got to go, it was nice seeing you and I hope you continue to have a good life."

Syb left me standing in the street. She hailed a cab and left me brokenhearted. My world came tumbling down. I almost cried standing there on that street. I walked to my car and I did cry once I got in. I just couldn't stop. Later when I had a clear mind, I realized the last nine months to a year had me close to a breakdown. I had to talk to someone, but it couldn't be Kit. She was worried enough about me, so I called my friend little Callie.

Callie answered Agnes's phone after one ring and she said, "Hello, Callie speaking."

I couldn't answer, I was choked up with tears. I began to cry like I've never cried before. Callie said, "Who is this? Father Mitch, is that you? Please answer me."

I choked out the words, "Yeah, it's me. I'm sorry Callie. I shouldn't be bothering you."

As I was fumbling to hang up, I could hear Callie yell, "Don't you dare hang up on me. Get back on this phone immediately."

I quietly said, "I'm here."

"You listen to me Father Mitch, and you listen good! You need me and I'm here for you. No one has ever helped me like you have. There is nothing you can say or do that will ever make me change my feelings for you. Now get your butt over here and pick me up. We're going to the lake Nokomis and talk about your problem. Okay?"

"Yeah, I need your help."

I sat for a while wondering what has happened to me. I'm calling a young girl that had so many bad things happen to her, to ask for advice. It should be me giving her advice. I then walked out to my car and drove to Agnes's house and Callie came running out. She said, "Hello Father Mitch, let's get to somewhere where we can talk in private. You look like shit, if you don't mind my language."

I said nothing but I did try to smile but I just couldn't. We parked the car and the walked to the park benches and sat down. Callie smiled and said, "Father Mitch, nothing can be this bad. We can work it out. I'm just guessing but I think you're about done being a priest, am I correct?"

"Yes, my young friend, I've about had it with the priesthood. I saw my old girlfriend Sybil and I realized that I still love her. She said she was seeing someone and didn't want to interfere with me potentially leaving the priesthood. She just said goodbye and walked away. This is about the third time she's done that. Oh Callie, I love her so. What shall I do?"

Callie smiled at me before saying, "Well, get off your lazy ass and go and get her. Father Mitch, I knew from the first moment I met you that you shouldn't be a priest. You have love in your heart for everyone and I could see right away you needed a woman. If I were your age, I'd have been after you right away. Now don't get me wrong, I'm in love with David and as soon as I get done with school, we'll get married. I'm going to stop calling you Father, from now on it's just Mitch. I love you so much and you are the father I never had."

"Callie that means so much to me that you think so highly of me. But if I leave the priesthood no one will like or respect me."

"Mitch, there are a few things that you don't know and I'm about to tell you. First, as you know your sister Kit and I have become great friends, we talk every day. For the last couple of months, it's been just about you. Kit and I both realized a long time ago you need to move on. By move on, I mean leave the priesthood. Kit has told your mom about this and she has come to the realization that the only reason you're a priest is because of her. She insisted on you going into the seminary and she knew she was wrong. She agrees you need a different life and you are not happy where you are now. Bud feels the same way. So now figure out how you will address the bishop when you tell him you're leaving. He was the guy that didn't back you up, wasn't he?"

"Yes, his name is Bishop Manning and I had his support for a while. I was having fun when I first got to St. Clement, but that all fell apart."

"Mitch, you were getting things done, something that had never been accomplished there before. You and I both know why nothing was ever accomplished before; it was because of the old men that run the church. They don't want anything to change. That Wiggins was stealing money from the church and you knew it. The church is run by old men that are set in their ways and it can't be changed. Look at what that bishop tried to do and what did it get him or you? You must leave the priesthood and you have the backing of all your family and friends."

I smiled at dear young friend and said, "You are wise beyond your years. I thank God every day that I met you."

"So, do I. But Mitch, your days of counseling are not over. You have the background and the education that will give you opportunities to do the same thing you're doing now but without the collar."

"I guess you're right. I should be able to find employment. I can't believe you know so much about me. I'm going to sleep on it tonight and make a decision tomorrow. Callie, you are the best and I love you more than you'll ever know."

The next morning, I called Bishop Manning's office and asked to speak to him. I was asked my name, which I told the receptionist. She quickly said the bishop was busy and couldn't be disturbed. I then said, "That's fine, just tell him I'm going to kill myself if he doesn't come to the phone."

That comment must have shook her up, 'Please don't do that, I'll get him right away."

Seconds later the bishop answered the phone and said, "Father Mitch, what are you doing? Trying to kill yourself is not what God wants, please get those thoughts out of your mind."

I replied, "I not going to kill myself now or later, it was the only way to talk to you. My guess is that the archbishop told you not to talk to me. Well I really don't care what he or you think anymore. I called to tell you I'm leaving the priesthood."

"Why would you do such a thing? You have such a wonderful future as a priest."

"Why, you ask? Why? Because it's run by a bunch of old fools that are so set in their ways and they can't think of the future. Do you realize that one third of the parishioners have left the parish of St. Clement? One third! Do you know why? It's because of Wiggins.

After that ham dinner where he stole all the money and demoted me, all the folks that worked on that dinner left the parish. Most were big donors and were happy someone came along and made friends with them. Wiggins never knew anyone's name or their background. I've been treated like shit around here. Yes, I said like shit."

The bishop said, "Please come over here and talk to me. I can see you're very upset and I want to talk when you've calmed down a bit. Please do this for me."

"Okay, I'll be there in a half hour."

"Father Mitch, I can't see you on such short notice. Let me look at my calendar. How about Friday around five o'clock?

"Friday at five o'clock you say? That's four days away, right?"

"Yes, that's the earliest I can fit you in.'

"Bishop Manning, I like you, but you are part of the problem. You have no balls to stand up to these old men. I'm sorry, Friday doesn't work for me. I'll talk to Wiggins today and I will resign today. This is exactly what Wiggins wants. And by the way, we raised thirty-six thousand dollars at that ham dinner. He reported it was seven thousand. Where do you think all that money went? Also, did you know that the esteemed Father Cole has a girlfriend? I saw him and her making out in her car in the church parking lot. It appeared she was dropping him off after their date. And the esteemed Father Basil has a boyfriend that is a Jesuit priest. Now, I don't know that as a fact, but many parishioners here at St. Clement have seen them together holding hands and smooching one another. You see Bishop, priests need someone too. Goodbye and good luck trying to change the culture of this archdiocese, in my opinion it can't be done."

"Wait Mitch, come over here right now, I cancel my other appointments."

"I will but after this conversation I know there is nothing you can say that will change my mind. If you still want me to come over, I will?"

"Yes, I'd like to see you before you resign."

I walked out to my old jalopy and got in and drove straight to St. Paul to the offices of the archdiocese. I walked up the staircase and asked for Bishop Manning. I was escorted to his office and he was standing there speaking to another priest. The bishop introduced me to a fellow priest named Father Rudsdil. We sat down and the bishop explained to Rudsdil that I was planning on leaving the priesthood. Rudsdil explained to me that the archdiocese has a program that they use to help wayward priests understand their commitment to the church. It would be held at a location where retreats are normally held and there would be three other priests there. He would take me right away.

I stood there stunned at what this man had said. I laughingly said, "You think I don't know what my commitment to the church is? But, what about the church's commitment to me? Everything I've done since I began my journey to become a priest was to honor my commitment to the church, but I never got the same commitment back from the church. All I've gotten was a lot of rhetoric back from old men telling me how I have to do what they tell me do and it's always the same old way. Nothing ever gets changed. People are different now than they were two thousand years ago. Change is a good thing for every church except the Catholic church. Don't you two ever ask yourselves why all the priests are leaving the church as well as all the parishioners? We have old men in Rome as well as here in Minnesota, telling us how to live our lives, while they sit in an ivory tower. And Wiggins, he actually thinks he's God. Well he is not, and that parish has gone from one thousand families to seven hundred in the short time I was there. Think about that and do the math, that's a thirty percent drop. What's the reason? Wiggins is the reason."

Rudsdil said, "It appears that you have made up your mind here. Too bad, I've heard that with some guidance you could become a good priest."

I looked at this fool standing in front of me and I said, "Guidance? You call what Wiggins did was guidance? If that was guidance, you had best kiss this church goodbye, because there will be a mass exit from the church in the future, mark my words. Goodbye to both of you, and please give my most sincere thanks to Wiggins for opening my eyes to where the church is headed." I walked out and headed to St. Clement to get my belonging and after that I was going to head home, where I belong.

HOME AT LAST

I went into the rectory and packed my duffle bag. I left all my priestly garments behind. I saw no one and that was fine with me. I'm sure the good bishop called Wiggins and told him I was leaving. As I walked towards my jalopy, there was Father Cole siting in the passenger seat of a car with a young woman. When I say young, she looked at least ten or fifteen years younger than him. I walked up to the car and I surprised both of them by knocking on the window. Cole rolled down the window and asked, "What do you want Collins?"

I smiled and replied, "Gotcha, didn't I? I told the bishop you had a girlfriend and sure enough you do. And you, young lady, you do know this man is a priest, and as so, he is supposed to be celibate. By the way you two were going at it pretty hard the last time I saw you. You were making out in this same car. I know now he's not celibate nor are you, young lady. You know you should be ashamed going after an old fart like this, you can do so much better." Cole was attempting to open the door and get out when I warned him, "You get out of that car and I'll kick your ass, you stupid old fart." He intelligently remained seated.

The look on his face was funny, he was in a panic mode and didn't know what to do. He quietly said, "You told the bishop? Why would you do that? This is none of your business or his."

"You bet your wrinkled old ass I told the bishop. Why did I do it; because you're a jerk and I can't believe you're a priest! And little girl, you better get as far away from this jerk as you can, he will bring you down. Goodbye to you, young lady, and Cole, I hope you rot in hell for what you're doing to this kid."

I felt so good after telling him off, so good. It was like twenty pounds was lifted off my chest. I got into my jalopy and headed for home.

When I stopped in front of the house my sister Kit ran out to greet me. She was followed by my mom. Kit got there first and hugged me, she said, Callie told me what you were planning. Did you do it?"

"Yes, I did it. I'm a free man. Hi Mom, I hope you're not too upset."

Mom said, "Not at all sweetie. We've been talking about this happening for several months now, it's about time. I'm to blame for all of this. I should never had insisted on you going to that damn seminary. Bud told me so a long time ago, I just wouldn't listen. Please forgive me."

I replied, "Mom, there is nothing to forgive. I needed to try it and it didn't work. Besides I got a free education out of it."

Mom hugged me and cried, we then walked up the sidewalk to the house when my friend Callie walked out of the house. She was all smiles and she also hugged me. What a reunion.

I was planning on moving into the basement apartment with Kit. However, Kit had moved down there a couple of years before and liked the privacy of it. She especially liked it because she and Mike could have alone time. I understood what she meant when she said, "Alone time."

I told her I'd stay upstairs and would find an apartment as soon as I found a job. This is not what I wanted. Having a bedroom next to my mother and Bud was going to be difficult. But I had no choice.

Kit told me she and Mike had planned on getting married in June and she had asked Callie to be her maid-of-honor. She told me long ago if I was still a priest, she wanted me to marry them. I told her I'd be at the wedding, but I would not partake in the ceremony in any way. This would be their event and I didn't want my presence to interfere with it.

Kit asked me many questions about what I was going to do and I just couldn't answer her. I just didn't know. I needed time to figure things out. She wanted to also know what I was going to do about Sybil. I told her I was going to do nothing. Syb had told me to stay away and I would stay away.

I decided to take some classes at the University of Minnesota in social services. I wasn't sure what I was qualified for, but I put together a resume that I didn't think was very impressive. I met with a guidance counselor at the admission office and went over my options. Her name was Joyce Jones and she was about my age and was very cute. In the short time since I left the priesthood, I realized I was more interested in women than ever before. As Joyce talked to me about my future, I wasn't paying any attention to her, I was looking at her face. Like I said, she was very cute.

Joyce interrupted my stare and asked, "Are you even listening to me?"

I was startled to say the least. I quietly lied, "I'm so sorry Joyce, but I have so much on my mind now, I was in deep thought." I really should have said, 'Joyce, I don't have anything on my mind but you and that cute little body of yours.' I don't think Joyce would have liked that, she seemed very serious.' So, I just sat there and smiled.

Joyce responded, "I understand you've made a big step leaving the priesthood but you need to concentrate. Contrary to what you believe, your resume is outstanding. I've never seen where a student had gotten their undergraduate degree in two and half years. Also, the four plus years of the Masters of Divinity program was completed in under three years. This resume is outstanding. So, what on earth would bring you to this university?"

I was pleasantly surprised at her comments and I was also a bit taken back. I replied, "I guess I just didn't know if I needed more education, and if not, what kind of job can I expect to find?"

Joyce said, "Mitch, you could teach, but you'd need to get a teaching degree, which would only take a short time. Or you could go into counseling immediately. I could recommend you to this university, we are in desperate need of counselors currently."

I again was surprised, I replied, "I'm not sure about that. There is one thing I sure of is, I'd like to buy you lunch."

Joyce quickly responded, "Are you hitting on me? If you are, stop it right now? I'm a married woman and I don't need any more of this crap from you or anyone else. What is wrong with you men? You all think every woman is interested in you, well they're not. Stay away from me, you ass."

My goodness did I screw up. I tried to respond by saying, "I'm so sorry Joyce, but you aren't wearing a wedding ring so I thought you were single. Please forgive me, I promise you'll never see me again."

I stood up to walk away and Joyce said, "Sit down Father Mitch. Yes, I said Father Mitch. I know you, but you don't know me. I go to church at St. Clement. You heard my confession many times. In fact, you helped me with some of my problems that I won't go into. That is why I was impressed with your resume. As a regular member of society now, you better learn how to adjust and talk to women. We are not sex objects; we are women that can think and make our own decisions. The last thing we need is for men to think they can have their way with us. I want to help you as you helped me, so let's talk."

I sat back down and was so embarrassed, I said, "Anything you want. I'm so sorry. Please, let's start over."

"My suggestion would be for you to look into counseling, but not here. Hennepin County is in need of counselors in their social services area. They are also in need of people to work in their Foster Care Adoption area. I can set up an interview for you with Mrs. Stanley who heads up the foster care area. Notice I referred to her as Mrs. Stanley, she's a beautiful woman and I don't want you to hit on her, she's married. She's married to my brother, as a matter of fact."

I lowered my head and said, "I'm so sorry. Let's forget all of this for the time being. I don't want to be reminded of what a fool I've been. Thanks Joyce, for your help. I'm afraid I need to learn to adjust to the outside world and I'm clearly not ready yet."

"Mitch, please come back and sit down. I'm also sorry I came on so strong. I know I can help you."

"Joyce, thanks, but no thanks, I need time to think about all that has happened to me lately. I didn't realize how screwed up I am. Forgive me for my indiscretion. I might be back some other time when I heal."

ON MY OWN AT LAST

I went home and asked my mom if I could borrow some money. I told her I needed a thousand dollars to get my own apartment. She agreed to my request and was puzzled why I would want to leave her home. I replied, "I need more privacy and I need my own space. Kit told me after she and Mike got married, Mike would move into the basement apartment with her. So, with that space being taken over by the two of them it was time for me to move along. Wish me luck Mom."

Mom hugged me and said, "We'll do whatever you ask. And Mitch, you never have to pay me back. Consider it part of your inheritance."

"Thanks Mom, but as soon as I get a job, you'll get the money back with interest. Love you."

Callie's boyfriend David Clough told me if I wanted a job in some sort of construction area his dad could help me find employment. He was a mechanic by trade but knew many in the construction businesses. He introduced me to a fellow named Jim Roesner who owned Roesner Construction in Bloomington. He needed what he called a gopher, to do all the dirty work. I told him I was qualified to be his gopher. My job was go to construction sites where the work had been completed and clean the mess up. They left dumpsters that I could fill up with the debris left behind. I was told that everything on the site could be thrown away and if I found anything of value, I could keep it. I also grew a beard and a mustache, which appeared to be the thing to do when entering the construction business.

I enjoyed the work and the solitude that came with it. I could forget all my problems and my past. I made some really good money and I was able to pay Mom off in the first month. I had gotten a small studio apartment close to work and I really enjoyed it. At some time in the future I knew I'd want a bigger place, but this place was fine for now. I enjoyed having my own place that I was responsible for. I made the rent payments on time every month and I kept the place in immaculate shape. I made my bed every morning and did my dirty dishes after eating every meal. I did go out frequently with Callie and Kit and sometimes their boyfriends joined us.

One very cold and snowy Saturday afternoon Callie, David and I went to a clothing store in Bloomington that sold winter coats, jackets, shoes and all other winter dressing apparel. I was trying on some winter boots for work when someone tapped me on the shoulder and said, "Mitch, do you remember me? I'm Joyce Jones and this is my husband Ralph."

I stood up and shook hands with Ralph and said, "Nice to meet you Ralph and it's nice to see you again Joyce."

Joyce said, "Looks like your buying some cold weather gear. Are you going hiking?"

"No, they're for work. I work construction now and it's damn cold when you work outside every day."

Just then Callie walked up and slid her arm around me and said, "Hi, I'm Callie."

I was about to introduce Callie when Joyce said, "I assume you're Mitch's girlfriend, I'm Joyce and this is my husband Ralph."

Callie giggled and said, "This old man is not my boyfriend but my father. Well not my father but my stepfather. My boyfriend is David, he's over there buying a new jacket. How do you know Mitch?"

Joyce smiled right back at Callie and said, "Yes Mitch is a bit old for you, nonetheless it wouldn't have surprised me if you two were together. He's a handsome man with that beard and mustache and you are a beautiful young woman. You do look familiar; do you attend church at St. Clement?"

"I did while Mitch worked there but I left when he did. I have not been back to a Catholic church since he left. I now go to an episcopal church here in Bloomington. Any church that doesn't want Mitch, doesn't want me either."

"Callie is my best friend and I look at her as a daughter or a younger sister. I won't go into details on how we met but let's just say we're very close."

David walked over to where we were all talking and he was introduced. Joyce said, "Do you ever get jealous of Callie and Mitch's relationship?"

David laughed and said, "What good would it do? It would be like me not being able to see my mom. Mitch is like her dad. She goes to him with all her problems and since I do too there's no jealously only a great friendship."

Joyce said, "Have you guys eaten? We're going down the street to the Dew-Drop-Inn for lunch, would you like to join us? It's just a hamburger joint but they are out of this world."

I answered, "You bet, I know exactly where the place is, I eat there all the time."

I drove my jalopy to the Dew-Drop-Inn and parked close to the door. Callie and David both got out and Callie, said, "Do you think Joyce wants to offer you a job?"

I replied, "I don't know and I don't care. I'm happy with what I'm doing right now. The work is monotonous and that's what I need now. Maybe in the summer I'll look for a better job with a career."

Joyce and Ralph were already sitting at a table when we walked in. We walked over and sat down. The small talk was good and nothing serious was being said. Thank God Joyce said nothing about a job. Our orders came and we all dove in. I had just taken a bite out of my very large hamburger when Joyce looked over my shoulder and said, "Why hello stranger. How are you?"

The woman said, "I'm good. This is my friend Les and you know my daughter Sam."

The voice sounded familiar, but I just couldn't place it. I turned around as Joyce was going to introduce us and saw it was Sybil. I stood up and quietly said, "Hi Syb, it's nice to see you again."

She looked me over and I'm sure the beard and mustache threw her off a bit. She said, "Mitch. I mean Father Mitch. How are you? This is my daughter Sammy or Sam, and this is my friend Les Houlton."

As I shook hands with Les, Joyce said, "Do you two know each other? Where did you meet?"

Callie smiled and interrupted Joyce, she said, "Hi Syb, I'm Callie and this is my boyfriend David. We're good friends with Mitch. He is no longer Father Mitch."

Joyce said, "You haven't answered my question, "You two know each other?"

Syb replied, "Yes Mitch and I lived two doors away as kids and we were very close friends."

Les said, "I'm a little bit jealous. Did you two date?"

Syb replied, "Yes, you could say that. Mitch was my first love."

Joyce said, "Would you guys like to join us?"

Les spoke up, "No, we'd like a table all to ourselves. Sorry. There's a table back in the corner Syb, let's take that one."

All of a sudden Sammy stood close to me and looked me in the eyes and said, "I know about you. Mommy tells me all the time you were her first and only love. Is that true?"

I turned to face Sammy directly and I said, "I don't know about your mommy, but she was definitely my first and only love. I don't know if you realize this, but you look just like your mommy did when she was your age. You're very pretty just like she was or is."

I could sense that Les was getting pissed off and he was beginning to fidget, putting his weight on one foot than the other. He snidely said, "I said, there's a table back there, let's take it."

Sammy slowly shook her head and quietly said, "Mommy, I'd like to eat here with Mr. Mitch and Miss Callie. I like both of them."

Syb looked at Les and said, "Would you mind Les, Sammy wants to sit here?"

"Yeah, you goddamn right I mind. I don't want to sit here with some old lover of yours. I thought you and I had something going here. Are you gonna let this little shit of a kid dictate where we're going to sit? Look, I'm paying for lunch, so we'll sit where I want to sit, understand?"

Syb was getting upset. I've known her almost all of my life and I can tell when she's pissed. She looked at Les with anger in her eyes and said, "You and no one else will ever call my daughter a little shit. We'll sit here with friends not back in the corner all alone. If you don't like it, I can pay for our own lunch."

Les was about to explode, he said forcefully, "Listen you bitch. I never did like that kid of yours and now I don't like you either. Goodbye and good riddance."

Syb replied, "Right back at ya meathead." As Les was walking further away Syb said, "That went well, don't you all think?"

Everyone at the table started to laugh and they all laughed long and hard. Even little Sammy was giggling so hard she said to her mom, "I have to go potty."

Syb took her hand and they headed to the ladies' room. After they were out of ear shot, Joyce said, "Do you two still have something for each other?"

Callie answered for me, "Yes they do. Well Mitch does and I bet Syb does too. She would never let that ass Les go if she didn't."

I just shrugged my shoulders. I didn't know how to respond. First off, I was surprised to see Syb and Sammy. I really liked that little Sammy. She was just like her mom, very feisty. And Syb, I just didn't know if she was interested in me or not. The way she left me back when I was contemplating leaving the priesthood left a bad taste in my mouth. I thought things were going pretty good for me now. Did I want her back in my life? Was I her last resort? I just sat there and stared straight ahead as Syb and Sammy sat down. Sammy sat right next to me. She smiled at me and said, "I don't like that Les, he's mean. I like you Mr. Mitch."

I smiled back at her and said, "I like you too Miss Samantha. Call me Mitch."

Syb said, "What's with the beard and stash? I liked you better without all of that."

Sammy jumped in, "I like your beard Mr. Mitch, it makes you look like a lumberjack. I have a book about lumberjacks and I like it when Mom reads it to me. You could come over sometime and read it to me."

"Is your real name Samantha? I like Samantha better than Sammy. What is your last name? And I like Mitch, instead of Mr. Mitch. Mr. Mitch makes me feel old."

Syb replied in a smug tone in her voice, "Her last name is Newman, the same as mine. And you are getting old. I guess I shouldn't have said that, I'm the same age as you are. Mitch, can you give us a ride home? Les drove us over here and it's my guess that he will not want to come back for us. Please!"

"Of course, I'll give you a ride. I'll have to take Callie and David home first."

Joyce chimed in, "We can give you a ride Syb, you live very close to our house."

Ralph had not said a word since we all sat down, he finally spoke up, "No, we're not giving Syb and Sammy a ride home Joyce. Wake up and smell the toast, Syb and Mitch want to spend some time together, don't you get it?"

I laughed at the look on Joyce's face. No, she hadn't gotten it. She was stunned and stuttered out the words, "Oh.... I get....it now. I'm so sorry Syb. Let's you and I get out of here Ralph."

I drove over to Mom's house and dropped off Callie and David. Callie smiled as she closed the door. I then asked Syb where she lived and she gave me the address. It took all of ten minutes to get there. They lived in an old apartment building in the suburb of Richfield. Rents in that area were cheap and the school district was not the best. Since Sammy was going on five, so she wouldn't start school for another year.

SYBIL NEWMAN???

We parked in front of Syb's apartment building and I said, "Well here we are. It was nice seeing you Syb and it was really fun meeting you Samantha. I should be going."

Syb had a look of surprise on her face as she said, "You're just leaving us off? I thought you could come in and we could talk a bit."

I took a deep breath and said, "I don't think that I should. You two look like you've got a pretty good life together, I don't think you need a retired priest to interfere with your lifestyle. I should just go."

Syb slowly got out of the car and was going to say something when Samantha said, "I like you Mitch. We don't care if you were a priest, I don't even know what that is, but Mom and I both like you. Won't you come in and read the lumberjack book to me?"

I looked at this little girl and saw a smile on her face, that said it all. She and her mom liked me.

How could I refuse? I said, "If your mom still wants me to come in I would sure like too."

Syb smiled and said, "I'd sure like that too. Follow us."

We got into the apartment and I looked around. It was as neat as a pin; nothing was out of place. I said to Samantha, "Who keeps this place so clean, is it you?"

"Mr. Mitch, Mom and I both work at cleaning it. She does most of it I guess, because I'm too little to do more of it. Do you like our place?"

I replied, "Please don't call me Mr. Mitch, please call me just Mitch. And, I love your apartment, it's really a nice place. Do you like it?"

"It's alright, but I'd like to live in a house like my friends do. I can't go out here and play, Mom worries someone might steal me."

"I think I can understand your mommy's feelings. How about I read you that book now. Your mom, you and I can all sit on the couch and I'll read the first few chapters. When I'm done Mom can take over."

"Goody, goody I can hardly wait."

The three us sat on that couch for over two hours reading and laughing. When it was time for dinner, Syb made us fried chicken, potatoes, and a salad. I hadn't had a home cooked meal in ages, so it was very good. After dinner we all cleaned up dishes and watched a Disney movie on TV. When it was time for Samantha to go to bed, she was so tired she couldn't stay awake long enough to complain. It was around nine o'clock when we closed the door to her bedroom when I said, "Well, I better get going too. It's been a long day."

Syb stood for a long while and stared at me without saying a word. She finally said, "You think you're going to get out of here that easy? I don't think so. I've waited all my life to get you alone and you think I'm going to let you out of here without making love with me? If that's what you think, well guess again buster?"

I laughed and said, "Make love? Really? It's been over fifteen years since I've made love and it was with you. Are you sure you want to? What if you get pregnant? You know I'd marry you, don't you? I'd also marry you if you weren't pregnant."

Syb grabbed my hand and said, "Follow me and stop rambling on about having babies. We're doing this for fun and you'll never know how horny I am."

"Horny, what's horny? Did I miss something?"

"Oh Mitch, you were in the priesthood too long. Horny means having strong sexual desires, or hot to trot with no place to race, or something like that. It's a slang that's been around for a long time. It's mostly guys that say their horny, but sometime us girls do to, and I'm horny right now. And, I'm horny for you and only you."

It took about three seconds for us to get all of our clothing off and another three seconds for me to explode. Syb laughed and held on to me so I couldn't roll away from her. I was embarrassed and she knew it. She finally was able to say, "No you don't. You're not getting away from me ever again. It was good for me knowing it was good for you. The next time it will be good for both of us. Remember foreplay? After you rest a bit, we'll have some foreplay, lots of foreplay. Mitch, I love you so much, I don't plan on ever letting you get away from me again."

I kissed her so many times that night that I thought maybe I had kissed to her too much. I began to apologize for too much kissing and she said, "You can never kiss me too much. I've waited for you so long we have to make up for lost time."

I finally asked her the question about getting pregnant. She replied, "I'm sorry for not answering that question before but I can't get pregnant again. I had a difficult time having Sammy and the doctor said it would likely kill me if I tried again, so he asked if he could tie my tubes and I agreed. I'm sure the Catholic Church would call that birth control of some kind but I'd rather be alive than dead after giving birth."

"I'm sure the church would not care in a situation such as that, but I'm not sure."

"Mitch, I need to know just how you feel about me and Sammy? Do you see us in your future?"

I smiled and shook my head yes and said, "You two are my future. Now after having sex with you again I'll never let you go ever again. And, as far as not being able to have more kids, I'm good with that. I think having Sammy will be a full-time job for both of us. I've been thinking about our future and I have lots of ideas that I want to run by you. But first, I think I can go one more time before I fall asleep."

"Me too, get over here."

Syb woke me at seven o'clock the next morning and said, "You better get dressed and start the coffee. I'll start breakfast as soon as I get dressed. I want it to look like you came over here early this morning. Mitch, you are the first man that I've had sex with since I got pregnant with Sammy. After I found out I was pregnant that's when my so-called husband disappeared."

Samantha woke up and was very excited to see me. She asked me if I stayed overnight and I lied and told her no. We all had breakfast together and teased one another until Sam laughingly said, "I've got to go potty."

I looked at Syb and said, "Does she always announce when she has to go to the bathroom?"

Syb smiled and said, "Why yes she does. It comes from when I was trying to train her. I told her to tell me when she had to go, and I'd help her. Well as you can see, she's trained but wants everyone to know she trained. She's just a goofy little kid."

"Just like her mom."

MARRIAGE, FAMILY & DEATH

Sybil, Samantha and I tied the marriage knot on July 3, 1983, both Syb and I had just turned thirty-three. We were married in an Episcopal Church called St. David's located in south Minneapolis. We knew the Catholic Church would not be interested in marrying us, so we picked a church that was. After our marriage we attended a Catholic Church called St. Kevin's also located in south Minneapolis. We had Samantha baptized there when she turned six years old. St. Kevin's became our church even though we knew we were not really welcomed there.

Our wedding was a simple, nice affair and Syb had my sister Kit as her maid of honor and I had my little friend Callie Gavrilo, aka Callie Clough as my best woman. Also, we had a little girl named Samantha as our flower girl. My mom cried almost through the entire ceremony. I could hear her say to Bud, 'I'm so sorry for what I did to Mitch, so sorry.' Our reception was at Mom's house in the backyard. Syb called her mother and left a message we were getting married and asked them to come. They didn't, however, call her back.

I thought it was quite unusual when my sister Kit and Mike Gorman were wed, I was not asked to participate in any of the ceremony, not even as an usher, which made me feel kind of left out. I felt left out because Kit and I were so close. However, when Callie got married, I was her man of honor. All the marriage ceremonies were fun and very festive. Syb and I celebrated all of them until we had to take Sam home and put her to bed.

It didn't take long for Sam to tell me she loved me and was happy I was her daddy. And, it didn't take me long to feel like she was my child and I became very protective of her. I adopted her before our marriage and she took my last name of Collins as did Syb.

When Sam entered first grade, we enrolled her in the St. Kevin's grade school and we also purchased our home close by. Syb continued to teach and I had gotten my first real job at Hennepin County working in the Foster Care Adoption area. Our friend Joyce Jones was instrumental in me getting that job. The nice part of the job was the flexible hours, so in the winter I could pick Sam up from school.

Things couldn't have been better for Syb and I during those first three years of our marriage. We loved each other so, and we could hardly wait to be together every evening. Sam was the nicest little girl I'd ever seen. She was compassionate toward other little kids and was very polite to adults, just like her mom. But all those things changed one night on a very snowy, winters night.

It was two weeks before Christmas and school would be out for Christmas vacation that Friday. Syb had scheduled her parent nights that week to go over her students' grades for the first semester. When she left for work that morning, she told me she'd be home around seven o'clock and I was to make the dinner for all of us. She insisted however, that I wait to eat with her as we always do. I smile and then kissed her as I said, "Yes dear, I'll wait for you. I love you."

She replied, "What would I ever do without you. I love you soooo much." Syb then kissed Sam and said, 'You be good and do what Daddy tells you to do. Love you."

Syb didn't get home at seven that night. I waited and waited and I finally heard a knock at my front door around nine o'clock. There were two police officers standing there and they asked, "Mr. Collins may we come in, it's about your wife Sybil."

I was petrified, I knew something bad had happened to my lovely wife. I was shaking when I opened the door wide so they could enter.

We sat down in the living room and I asked, "What has happened to my wife? Is she okay?"

The officer in charge cleared his throat before saying, "There has been an accident and your wife is dead. An old man ran a red light and plowed into your wife's car. We believe she died instantly, but we're not sure. As you know it's a slippery night and the old man didn't see the stop sign. Your wife's remains have been sent to the Hennepin County morgue. Mr. Collins we are so sorry to have to tell you this horrible news and we're sure you would have liked to have someone other us delivery this tragic news to you. If there is anything, we can do for you please call me at this number. My name is officer Francis."

The two officers left me alone and I cried my eyes out. I don't know how long I sat there but it was quite a while. The doorbell rang and I peeked out the window and there was Callie. I opened the door and Callie jumped into my arms crying like a baby. She was crying so hard I couldn't understand anything she was saying. Finally, she calmed down and said, "It was on the news about Syb, oh Mitch this just can't happen to you two. You loved each other so much. No, this can't happen. I'm so sorry, what can I do?"

We both sat on the couch and cried. There were more people at my front door and in between bawling out loud I opened the door and there was Kit and my mom. The crying didn't stop until my daughter Samantha walked out of her bedroom wiping the sleep form her eyes and said, "Where's Mommy? Grandma, auntie Kit, auntie Callie, why are you all here? Where's my mommy?"

I picked Sam up in my arms and I took her back to her bedroom and explained what had happened. That was the hardest thing I'll ever have to do in my life. Tell a child her mommy has just died. I held her in my arms until she cried herself to sleep. I tucked her in and returned to the living room. Callie said she was going to stay with me and Sam. I told Mom and Kit to go home and I'd see them both tomorrow.

The next day my mom took care of Sam as Callie and I went to McDevitt's funeral home to set up a burial for my Syb. It took us over two hours to complete the arrangements. The funeral would take place in two days and she would be buried at Lakeside Cemetery.

I picked up Sam at my mom's and she wasn't talking to anyone including me. I took her by the hand and we walked to my car. Once in the car Sam said, "Are you still going to be my daddy or am I going to be adopted by someone else?"

That broke my heart. I cried while saying, "You are always going to be my little girl. No one else will ever be your daddy, just me. Sam, I love you so much, just as much as I loved Mommy. No one will ever take you away from me." Sam crawled over to me and hugged me for a very long time while we both cried.

After out embrace she said, "Daddy, I'm hungry, can we go to the place where Mom and I first met you?"

I laughed and said, "Yes, we'll go there. But Sam, I met your mom when we were in grade school. It was love at first sight."

"I know. Mommy told me she loved you all her life. Will you love me all your life?"

I cried again at her question and I replied, "I promise there will never be a day that I don't tell you how much I love you. You will be loved so much you'll get sick of me telling you how much I love you. Now, let's get some lunch."

Sybil's wake was on a Thursday night in the middle of winter. It was so cold my jalopy wouldn't start. David and Callie came over and jumped started the jalopy. David quietly said to Callie, "I hope he knows this piece of shit is on its last legs."

I replied, "I heard that! Don't you know it's your job to keep it running? It's old but reliable."

David yelled, "Reliable! You think this old junk heap of metal is reliable? Why are we here in the freezing cold to try and start it? I'm sick and tired of taking care of your old cars, and as a matter of fact, I'm sick and tired of you calling my wife every time something goes wrong in your life. And it seems that some things go wrong almost every day. I'm sick of this crap and so is she. After today please don't call us again. I'm done helping you out and I don't want you abusing my wife's friendship anymore. Have you got it? This all ends today. I'm sorry you lost your wife but grow a pair, it's not the end of the world. Bury her and move the hell on."

Callie was about to say something and I cut her off. I replied, "Thanks for all your help David, I understand your frustration, it won't happen again. And Callie, he's right, I relied on you way too much. I'm on my own now and I promise you both I will not bother you ever again."

Callie had tears running down her cheeks and she attempted to say something, but I cut her off again. I said, "I've got to go."

I walked into my house and got Sam and we got into the car and headed to the wake.

When we got to the funeral home Mom, Kit and Mike were there. We had agreed upon a closed casket since Syb's body was not a pretty sight. I also didn't want Sam seeing her mommy like that. The casket was in front of the room and there were chairs set up for people to sit down. The first two people to walk in were Syb's mother and dad. They walked over and said a prayer in front of the closed coffin. Afterwards they strolled over to where Sam and I were standing and Mrs. Newman hugged me and Mr. Newman shook my hand. They looked at Sam and Mr. Newman said, "Hello Samantha, we're your grandparents. We would like you to come and live with us? Would you like that?"

I quickly said, "No, she would not like that. You are complete strangers to her and you both shunned your daughter, so why come here now? You should have come to our wedding if you wanted to see us. But now, when Syb's dead you come in here and want my child?"

Mrs. Newman replied, "You are in no position to raise a young girl, I am. I raised a daughter and she worked hard and got a college degree. If it weren't for you, she likely be alive today. It was you that ruined her life and forced us to disown her. But we will not do that to our granddaughter."

I smiled at both of them and said, "Let's ask Sam where she wants to live, we'll leave it up to her."

Sam said, "I don't want to live with you. I'm living with my daddy."

Mr. Newman said, "Well I've gotten an attorney and we'll get custody of her, count on it. She's nothing to you, not even a blood relative."

"No, she not a blood relative, but she is my daughter. I have adopted her and now she is my child. I suggest your attorney contact Hennepin County, that is where the adoption took place. Now both of you get the hell away from me, my daughter and my dead wife. If you wanted to make amends you should have done so while Syb was alive. Coming in here and demanding to take my daughter away is not making amends. If sometime in the future you want to spend time with my daughter you may, but at our home."

After the Newman's had left the funeral home, Kit laughed and said, "Boy, the balls on those two. Aren't you glad you went through the adoption?"

"Yeah I am. Kit, I'm not in a very good mood tonight because I had a run in with David and Callie. It seems like I've taken advantage of Callie and her friendship with me. I don't want to talk about this right now, but I think I'm off their Christmas list."

People began to pour in, and I knew most of them. There were kids that had been students of Syb's with their parents. Other teachers showed up and I was impressed by all the people that knew and loved my dear wife.

One couple I didn't know approached me as the wake was about over. The male said, "Hi, you must be Mitch? My name is Tyler Garrod and I am Sybil's ex-husband. I'm so sorry for your lost. This is my wife Carin. We need to talk with you about Sammy when the time is right."

"What is it that you want to discuss about Sammy. Right now, is as good a time as ever."

"Well I'm not sure this is the place to discuss this."

"Mr. Garrod, this will be the only place or time I'll discuss Sammy with you and your wife, so speak up."

"Well okay, if you insist. I want custody of my daughter. My wife and I are unable to have children and since Sammy is my biological child, I'm going to pursue custody of her."

I had enough of these people and Syb's parents who all wanted to take my daughter away from me. I looked at this idiot and said, "First off, you explicitly told Syb that Sam was not your child. Did you forget that? You said she was fooling around with another guy. Don't you remember that? And you Mrs. Garrod, didn't you go and ask Syb to divorce her husband so you could have him? Does any of that sound familiar to either one of you? Let me explain something to the both of you, so I can save you some money on attorney fees. I adopted Sam before Syb and I got married. Go to Hennepin County and check it out. Sam is my child and you two clowns have no rights to her now or ever. I won't tolerate either of you making contact with her ever again, if you do, I'll get a restraining order against both of you. Now get away from me and my family."

Mrs. Garrod began to cry as they walked out hand in hand.

I walked over to where Sam was standing with my sister Kit and said, "Let's go home baby girl. It's going to be a long day tomorrow."

As Sammy grabbed my hand, Callie walked up to me with David standing way behind. She said, "I know you're mad at us, but David has had enough of our constant friendship. He's jealous and rightly so. Sometimes I do more with you than with him. I'm sorry but I'm married and have a child, I need to spend my time at home. I hope you understand."

"I do and thanks for telling all of this. Your timing is impeccable, just what I needed and wanted at my wife's wake. Goodbye to you and Davy, you make a great pair. Please stay away from me and please stay away from the funeral service tomorrow. You two are the last people I need to see."

EPILOGUE

Syb's funeral at St. Kevin's was short and sweet. I got up and said a few words and told everyone how thankful Samantha and I were that they all came. I said after the burial we would have a small lunch served in the basement of the school. The limo drove Sam, Mom, Kit, Mike and I to the graveyard. The priest said a few prayers and Syb would be placed in the ground later. After everyone had left the site, I stood alone there by the grave with tears running down my cheeks. I was wondering what I do without Syb when a hand gently grabbed mine. I looked up and it was Callie. She was crying. The two of us stood together holding hands for the longest time. Callie finally said, "Please forgive me. You and I have been through so much together and have helped each other through so many rough times. If David doesn't understand that, then he'll have to divorce me. I told him before we got married about our friendship and how you were like a father to me. I made it clear last night I wasn't going to leave you. I love you so much. The things you did for me, no one else could have done. You never judged me, you only supported me. Without you I couldn't have made it. What my father did to me was so terrible and horrific and you were always there to tell me it wasn't my fault. Mitch, I need you to forgive me."

"There is nothing to forgive. I realized last night I've relied on you too much. I love you like I love Sam, like my daughter. You have always been there for me through thick and thin. You've never wavered. So, don't let David divorce you, you need each other. I'll still stay in touch, but not like we have in the last ten years. I hope that is okay with David, I don't want to lose you for good?"

"I'm telling you right now, I won't allow him to tell me when and where I can talk to you. If I need you every day then it will be every day. Our relationship is never going to change I promise you that. You'll need me more now than ever before and I plan on being there for you."

"What would I do without you. I thought about you all last night, wondering if you'd ever talk to me again. I guess we just need one another. Losing Syb this last time has taken its toll on me. I guess I need a friend more than ever. Let's go and eat lunch and talk about Syb."

After the lunch Sam and I went home to an empty house. I drowned my sorrows in a glass of coke and Sam did too. After we finished our beverages my beautiful little daughter said, "Daddy, I heard what you said to those people that said they were my grandpa and grandma. You wouldn't let them take me. I also heard you say to that man that said he was my daddy, that he couldn't have me either. I love you Daddy; you always take good care of me. We're going to miss Mommy, aren't we?"

"Yes sweetie, we are. But Mommy would want us to keep going and to live our lives like she was still with us. We'll do alright you just wait and see."

It was only two days after Syb was buried that Callie stopped by one night to say hello. I could tell she had been crying and was very upset. I asked what was wrong and she blurted out, "David has left me and little Kathleen. He said he couldn't stand me any longer and had found a new love. He wants a divorce. I didn't know this, but our house is in foreclosure and he hadn't made any payments in the last six months. His dad's auto shop is going bankrupt. I knew business was bad, but his dad had told David he'd have to learn to do more things, but he had refused. He told me it was all over his head and he just didn't understand it like his dad did. You saw him the other day at your house. He's been mean to me and Kathleen like he was to you all the time now. And can you believe he has a girlfriend? I found a picture of her in his wallet while he was sleeping and she's homely. When I say homely, I mean really homely."

I laughed and asked, "What are your plans? Is he leaving the house, or are you?"

Callie replied, "Kathleen and I are leaving. That's why I'm here. Can we stay here for a while? I can pay some rent but not much. I promise I'll help out with everything and I'll also babysit for Sam."

"Oh Callie, I'm so sorry for the way David is treating you. I didn't see that coming. I always thought he was such a nice guy. As far as staying here, of course you can. You'll not pay a cent. Having you guys around will make things easier for Sam and me."

Callie was crying again and I held her in my arms and said, "Listen it's not the end of the world. We'll both get by. I'll tell you another thing, I'm planning on selling this house. There are too many memories here. Both Sam and I think a change of scenery would be good. I'm going to look into buying the double bungalow down the street, and you and Kathleen could move into the other side. We'd all have our privacy. What do you think?"

"Can we move in here this week? I know it's so soon after Syb's death, but I need to get out of that place, it's not good for Kathleen to hear all that bickering."

"We'll get Mike and Kit to help us move you and we'll get you out of there next week. In the meantime, you two can get what you need out of the house and move in here right away."

Kathleen was only a year younger that Sam and they were already good friends. Both attended St. Kevin's school and they had some of the same friends. This arrangement would work out for all of us.

Callie and Kathleen moved in with us and never left. I did buy the double bungalow and we shared it with Callie and Kathleen. I went to work for the University of Minnesota as a guidance counselor and stayed there until I retired. I did come back to the Catholic Church.

I taught Sunday school and I also taught religious instructions for potential Catholics. Sam graduated from the University of Minnesota with a degree in education, like her mother had. She married a young man named Maurice McInerny who became a doctor. They have two children both boys; one named Mitchell after me and one named Michael after Mike Gorman.

My mother lived a long full life and passed away at the ripe old age of eighty-nine. Bud had passed away ten years before Mom. They had a very nice life together. My sister Kit and her husband Mike stayed married and they have three kids two girls and a boy. The boy was named after me and the girls were Bridget after Mom and Callie after my best friend Callie.

I never regretted leaving the priesthood. I just couldn't believe in all they wanted me to believe. But I have a firm foundation for my faith. I believe in Jesus Christ and all he taught about love and forgiveness.

By leaving the priesthood I was able to be a husband and a father, two things that turned out to be the most important things in my life. God truly blessed me and I thank Him every day for all he has given me. This is the story of my life; it was a good life and I'm happy for every part of it. God Bless!

ACKNOWLEDGEMENTS

To my wife LaVonne Snyder Mountain, for her creative work on the covers and for her constant encouragement and for all her support over the last 55 years. To my son Patrick M. Mountain, for his encouragement and his contributions that made the distribution of my books possible. To my other sons, Mark W. Mountain and Scott C. Mountain, for all their constant encouragement and support. To my daughter-in-law Emilia Poppe Mountain and to my only grandchild William B. Mountain for all their love and support.

Also to one of my family members that has been instrumental in getting my books distributed, my wonderful niece Jill Martin. Jill did all the formatting, structuring and editing of my last five books. Without her expertise and her help none of these books would have been completed. Jill has a very demanding, successful career, but she still finds time to help an old man like me out. She is loved and greatly appreciated by me and the rest of my family.

I would also like to thank several of my close friends that have always encouraged me to continue writing, they are as follows; Peter Schenk, Harry Daly, Scott Hutton, Ron Naslund, Ted Boran, Jerry Guptil and Roger Young.

Also, to my dear friends that have helped with the editing, Carol Gorman and Barb Donley. To my old buddy Larry Podobinski for all his help in editing and for his encouragement. Last, but not least, to my very **old** friend Mike Gorman. Mike had read only two books in his life prior to reading five of my books and he passed both the oral and written exams I gave him. He's a strong 'C' student now. Mike's name has appeared in all of my books in some shape or form, but in a most complimentary way.

ABOUT THE AUTHOR

I was born and raised in Minneapolis, Minnesota and have lived there for all but the nine years my family and I spent in the Boston area. After a trip to my family's hometown Killeagh, Ireland, I became interested in writing and researching my family's genealogy. That inspired me to write the fictional trilogy of my family, The Saga of the Brothers Mountain, William, and WJ American Hero.

In addition to the family trilogy, I have written the following fictional books: Padraig Murphy, Foster Lake, Will Cobb, The Hunt for Kevin Hart, The Legend of Annie Crow and Mitchell Collins.

My new book, Mitchell Collins was inspired by my Catholic education and all the doubts I had because of it.

My wife LaVonne and my sons Patrick, Mark, and Scott have been instrumental in encouraging me to write and complete my books.

For more information, visit www.mwmountain.com.

Made in the USA
Monee, IL
20 July 2024